# Gunflame

# Gunflame

## WAYNE D. OVERHOLSER

**Sagebrush**
Large Print Westerns

**Library of Congress Cataloging in Publication Data**

Overholser, Wayne D., 1906-
   Gunflame / Wayne D. Overholser.
      p.     .cm.
   ISBN 1-57490-251-2 (alk.paper)
  1. Large type books.  I. Title.
PS3529.V33 G78 2000
813'.54—dc21                                         99-054891

Cataloging in Publication Data is available from the British
Library and the National Library of Australia.

**Sagebrush Large Print Westerns** are published in the
United States and Canada by Thomas T. Beeler, Publisher,
Box 659, Hampton Falls, New Hampshire 03844-0659.
ISBN 1-57490-251-2

Published in the United Kingdom, Eire, and the Republic of
South Africa by Isis Publishing Ltd, 7 Centremead, Osney
Mead, Oxford OX2 0ES  England. ISBN 0-7531-6249-0

Published in Australia and New Zealand by Bolinda Publishing
Pty Ltd, 17 Mohr Street, Tullamarine, Victoria, 3043, Australia.
ISBN 1-86340-008-4

Manufactured by Sheridan Books in Chelsea, Michigan

# Gunflame

# CHAPTER 1

## Man in Love

SIX YEARS OF RIDING WITH MATT WILDEW HAD taught Rick Malone many things about the gunman. Wildew was a killer, a professional who wore his .44 in a tied-down holster on his right hip, a man whose blinding speed on the draw was never hampered by the burden of an exacting conscience.

Yet, paradoxically, Rick had learned that Wildew seemed to have his own strict code. As long as Rick had known him, his word had been his bond; his working agreement was a contract which he had never violated. When he took his job, his soul went with his gun.

Now, lying on his side in the Bent R bunkhouse, Rick watched Wildew playing solitaire on a table across the room from him. Rick thought of the last six years, and of the things the gunman had tried to teach him. He had learned some of them, and now he thought of the lessons he had not learned. To the extent he had failed to learn them, he was a disappointment to Wildew, and he was glad of it.

"The damned cards won't come up," Wildew said angrily as he swept them off the table and began to shuffle. "That makes three times in a row I've lost."

"You can't beat your luck when it's running bad," Rick said.

"That's right, kid." Wildew laid the cards down. "Our luck turned on us all around. It's been a good job, though. Good pay, good grub, and no real hard work. Now it's over, looks like."

1

Rick sat up and rolled a smoke. They had not talked about their plans since Vance Spargo had been shot. Now it was time, and Rick knew how it would be. Wildew would drift on just as he had for years, but Rick was staying, and it was going to be hard to tell him.

"Yeah, reckon it's over," Rick agreed, and fired his cigarette.

Wildew pinned his pale blue eyes on Rick's face. He was forty-six, a slender man with a narrow, deep-lined face and a fringe of white at the temples. Rick often thought of him as a machine devoid of emotion. Or at least it seemed so when he chose to hide his thoughts and feelings behind expressionless eyes as he did now.

"Funny thing about a man like Vance Spargo," Wildew murmured. "He spends years building an outfit like Hatchet. Gets so damned big he don't have to answer to nobody, but when his time comes, a slug cuts him down same as it does a little fellow."

Rick got up and moved to the bunkhouse door. Twilight had given way to night, and the faint glow of scarlet lingering above the western rimrock would soon be gone. From where he stood Rick could see the lighted lamp in old Lou Rawlins' office window. The rest of the ranch house was dark, but Nan, Lou's granddaughter, was there, somewhere, waiting for the last light to fade. Then Rick would meet her in the pines back of the house.

He hated it, this hiding and dodging and hoping that Rawlins wouldn't find out they were in love. Now it would have to come out. With Vance Spargo dead, the old man would have no further use for a pair of gunhawks.

"We've never been in Arizona," Wildew said tentatively. "Tucson would be a good place to spend the winter."

2

"I ain't going," Rick said.

Wildew was silent for a moment. Rick, standing with his back to the gunman, could hear the whisper of his breathing, and he felt the faint stirring of regret. When you ride with a man for six years, you form habits that are hard to break. You know what to expect; you learn the other's weaknesses and strengths, and when the chips are down, you know the kind of odds you can accept and still come out alive, providing you have an average run of luck. That was the point. Rick had had better than average luck from the time he had thrown in with Wildew. Sooner or later it would turn sour. Rick had seen it happen, and he'd heard Wildew talk about gunfighters who wound up in boothill because something had gone wrong. If a man lived by the gun long enough, he died by the gun. It was the natural destiny of men like Matt Wildew, but it was not the kind of finish Rick had wanted. Not after falling in love with Nan Rawlins.

"You like it here?" Wildew asked softly.

"That's it. I'm going to go to work."

"Now that's a hell of an ugly word," Wildew murmured. "Counter jumping maybe while you starve to death saving enough dinero to impress Lou?"

"No. I'll get a job on a ranch."

"Not on the Bent R you won't," Wildew said. "When the old boy finds out you've been making calf eyes at Nan, he'll kick your seat from here to Bald Rock."

"Then I'll get a job on some other spread. Nan will wait for me."

"It's great to be young and in love." Wildew rose and walked to the door. "You and me have been together a long time, kid."

Rick turned. Wildew's face was as expressionless as

ever, but he sensed the feeling that was in him, as much feeling as the gunman was capable of having. Rick said, "I know, Matt. I'm beholden to you, but I don't see no future in our way of living. I'm going to break it off clean."

"For thirty a month and found," Wildew said contemptuously. "We can get work in Arizona, kid. There's always trouble along the border, and folks who are in trouble need a pair like us."

Rick shook his head. "I can't do it, Matt."

He stepped outside, knowing that Nan would be waiting for him. Wildew said, "Wait, Rick."

Rick turned. "No use augering about it, Matt. I know what I've got to do."

"I ain't augering," Wildew said mildly. "Just wanted to say I'll hang around a few days. Something might turn up."

"Not with Spargo dead. Lou will move in on Hatchet range as soon as they plant Spargo."

"There's the Diamond J," Wildew reminded him. "And Grant Jenner. You never know about setups like this. Throw a bone to a couple of mean dogs and they'll fight over it."

"Not Jenner," Rick said, and left the bunkhouse.

He walked past the kitchen door. There were still just the two lighted lamps, the one in the bunkhouse and the other in Lou's office, their long yellow fingers thrown out across the hard-packed earth of the yard. He thought of Nan wanting a lawn and some flowers, and how Rawlins had laughed at her, saying she'd better move to town if she wanted stuff like that.

He moved around the woodshed toward the pines, his mind turning to Grant Jenner and his Diamond J. It lay across the river, a fair-sized spread about as big as the

4

Bent R. Both had suffered from Spargo's bullying, and they had thrown in together to make the fight against Hatchet, but alongside tough old Lou Rawlins, Grant Jenner was as soft as custard pudding.

Without Lou to stiffen his backbone, Jenner would have sold out when Spargo had given them his ultimatum last spring. No, Wildew was crazy. There would never be any trouble between the Bent R and Jenner's Diamond J. They'd divide Hatchet range and hold it if they could, with old Lou the big gun on Pine River as he had been years ago and wanted to be again.

"Rick."

He was almost in the pines when he heard Nan's low call. He quickened his steps when he heard her. She came to him, her hands outstretched. He took them, looking down at her, his love for this slim, blonde girl rushing through him like a hot breath of flame.

"You're slow, Rick," she whispered. "I've been waiting for five minutes."

"I'm sorry. I was talking to Matt."

He kissed her, her arms coming up around his neck and clutching him with fierce longing. There was this moment of sweetness when all his doubts and problems were swept away. Just the two of them, and Lou Rawlins with his greed and longing for power did not exist.

She drew back, saying softly, "I love you so much, Rick. Sometimes I can't believe it's possible."

He laughed. "I think the same thing. I don't believe it's happened to me."

She gripped his arm. "But it has, Rick. It has. Don't let anything destroy it."

He knew what she meant. She had told him more than once that if he kept on with Matt Wildew he'd wind up just like the gunman, tough and incapable of loving anything or anyone. A killing machine! That was the name she had for Wildew and she was right.

"Nothing can destroy it," he said fiercely. "Matt wants to light out for Arizona. I told him I was staying."

"What did he say?"

"He didn't like it." Rick took a long breath. "I feel kind of bad about it. We've been together quite a spell."

She pulled her arm back. "You've got to decide, Rick. We've been over this so many times."

"I have decided," he said quickly. "It wasn't no hard decision to make, but Matt did say one thing that made sense. He claims Lou will kick me from here to Bald Rock when he finds out about us."

"Then he'll kick me, too," she cried. "He ran Daddy's life when he was alive and he's run mine up till now. It's time I was living the way I want to live."

"I haven't saved much," he said miserably. "Just a few hundred dollars. I can't support you on a cowboy's wages."

"Then I'll work, too. Listen, Rick. I've seen women wait for their men, just wait and hope and get old. I won't do it. There's no reason to wait because I've got a stubborn old granddad who's got his notions about who I'm going to marry. Let's tell him now, Rick. He might as well start getting used to it."

"We'd better wait till after Spargo's funeral."

"Wait," she said scornfully. "That's all we've been doing. We should have got married a month ago. The day you told me you loved me. Remember?"

He remembered all right. It was not something a man would forget. He had been riding along the north rim watching the valley below the Bent R. Rawlins had been afraid Spargo would raid the Bent R, so he had stationed

6

Rick on the rim and had kept Wildew at the house.

Spargo had never made the attack Lou had expected, although it might have come if Lou had not hired Rick and Wildew. The three Bent R hands were with the cattle in the high country near the head of Pine River, and that had left the headquarters ranch wide open.

It had been just another late spring day until Rick had stopped at a creek for a drink and Nan had ridden out of the timber. He was not sure yet whether their meeting had been an accident, but he had a feeling she had been watching for him. Either way, it was the first time he'd had a chance to see her alone.

He had been in love with her from the first week he had been on the Bent R. He had considered it a hopeless love, the kind a man rides away from because the girl is as far out of reach as the moon. But he had blurted out his feelings in a tumbling, almost incoherent flow of words, and she had said quite simply, "You've been blind, Rick, or you'd have seen I felt the same way."

He said now, "Sure I remember. It was the biggest day of my life. All right, Nan, we'll go tell him if you want it that way."

She laughed shakily. "I'm not sure I want to hear what Grandpa's going to say, but we've got to do it."

They started toward the house, Rick holding her hand, a feeling of futility working through him. This was not the kind of problem he knew how to meet. If it were a matter of violence, of force against force, he could handle it. Six years of traveling with Matt Wildew had trained him to meet problems of that kind, but with something like this Wildew would be as helpless as he was.

They reached the woodshed when they heard a man ride up. Rick said, "Wait. Let's see who it is."

7

"Grant Jenner probably," she said. "He might as well hear it, too."

Still he hesitated, not wanting to talk in front of Jenner. He heard the man step up on the porch, a board squeaking under foot, and heard him knock. A moment later Rawlins said, "Oh, it's you, Kinnear," in a fretful voice as if he wished it was anyone else.

Joe Kinnear was the district attorney of Chinook County, a handsome, smooth-tongued man who made no secret of his political ambitions. Rick did not know him well, but he instinctively distrusted him as he did all lawyers, and he knew that Rawlins felt the same way.

"What does he want?" Nan whispered.

"Hard to tell," Rick answered.

But he thought he knew. Vance Spargo's murder was the biggest thing that had ever happened in Chinook County. He had been shot in the back, and Rick still had no idea who had pulled the trigger. It wasn't Wildew, for he would never kill a man that way. Possibly it had been one of Grant Jenner's gunhands. He had hired a pair, the same time Rawlins had hired Rick and Wildew, but Jenner was hardly the kind of man who would order a killing. Either way, the law would suspect Lou Rawlins or his men as much as Jenner's bunch until there was definite evidence.

For a moment Rick hesitated, then he heard Rawlins shout, "To hell with you. Get out of here." And Kinnear shout back, "Don't be a fool, Lou. You've got to deal with me."

"Stay here," Rick said, and ran around the house to the front door.

Lou Rawlins had brought the lamp from his office and had set it on the ancient pine table in the middle of

8

the living room. Now he stood at one end of the table, a tall gaunt man with wiry white hair that was never in place five minutes after it was combed, and a square-cut beard that jutted forward from a wide chin. His eyes, once dark blue, had faded until they were almost colorless, and his face, weathered by wind and sun until it was as dark and grim as the rimrock that flanked the valley, was filled with hatred.

Joe Kinnear stood with his back to the door, a tall, heavy-shouldered man who had been raised on a down-valley farm and had not let town life soften him. Neither Rawlins nor Kinnear was aware of Rick's presence. For a moment he stood there, watching, not sure whether this called for interference.

Then Rawlins found his voice. He bawled, "Threaten me, will you? Why, you thieving, mealy-mouthed, walking law book, I'll bust you so flat you won't be able to turn a page."

"You'll deal with me," Kinnear said in a low tone, "or you'll go to jail for the murder of Vance Spargo."

That was too much for Rawlins. He jumped at the lawyer, gnarled fists swinging wildly. Kinnear took one step forward and starting his right below his belt, caught the old man squarely on the point of his chin and knocked him down.

Rick lunged forward, grabbed Kinnear by the shoulder and swung him around. He hammered the lawyer on the nose with a jolting right; he felt the nose flatten under his fist and Kinnear went back, surprised and dazed. Rick was on him, giving him no chance to recover, nailing him with rights and lefts that rocked Kinnear's head from one side to the other.

Kinnear was a heavier and stronger man. Now he lunged at Rick, taking another punch on the side of his

9

head, and he got his hands on Rick. He smothered Rick's punches, wrestling him back across the room, and brought a short sledging blow into Rick's stomach that sent a spasm of pain through him.

They stumbled over a chair and went down in a tangle of legs and arms, Rick hearing Nan's voice in a high, protracted scream. He jumped clear and regained his feet, backing away as he struggled for breath.

Kinnear came up slowly from the floor, a dribble of blood flowing from his nose. He grabbed up the chair and threw it and lunged after it. Rick ducked the chair and met Kinnear's rush with an impact that shook the pictures on the wall, and again he slashed Kinnear's blood-smeared face with a sledging right. Kinnear, caught off balance, fell back against the wall and slid down to the floor.

For a moment Kinnear lay there, staring blankly at Rick as if not seeing him clearly, then he dug inside his frock coat for a gun. Rick swung a foot, kicking Kinnear's wrist and sending the gun spinning across the floor. Kinnear grabbed Rick's foot and brought him down in a hard, loose-jointed fall.

Kinnear lost his grip on Rick's foot. Rick went over the lawyer in a swift, cat-like motion and came again to his feet before Kinnear could get up and reach him. Now Rick moved in and Kinnear retreated, head dropped forward on his big shoulders, lips flattened against white teeth, arms up in a vain effort to protect himself.

Rick pursued him coldly and relentlessly. The lawyer backed into the table, shoving it behind him, legs screeching on the rough floor. Rawlins grabbed the lamp and jumped away, then the table went over with a crash.

Kinnear braced and held his ground, and Rick, close now, hammered his jaw with a brutal, driving right. Kinnear fell forward and clutched Rick with both arms. He hung on, burying his face against Rick's chest, his knees giving under him, full weight on Rick.

Rick hit him on the side of the head and then again. Still the lawyer hung on; he braced himself on rubbery knees and brought his head upward, striking Rick on the chin. Light exploded across Rick's eyes and he went back, breaking free from Kinnear's grip. The lawyer lurched forward, hands outstretched, and Rick slammed a hard left to the man's jaw. Kinnear fell flat and lay motionless, his arms flung out.

"Quite a fight, kid," Wildew said from the front door. "Quite a fight for a man who's got a gun for sale."

Rick staggered across the room to a leather couch and sat down. For a moment the room spun crazily before his eyes, the floor buckling like the surface of a lake caught in a high wind. Nan ran to him, crying, "Rick, are you all right?"

"Sure, I'm all right," he muttered.

She dropped down beside him, a hand reaching for his. The room quit spinning; Rick saw Wildew standing in the doorway, a cigarette in the corner of his mouth, smoke making a faint shadow before his face. Rick knew what he was thinking. He'd said over and over, "If you aim to make a living with your gun, never use your fists on a man." It was one of the lessons Rick had not learned.

Rawlins set the lamp on the floor and bringing the table upright, picked up the lamp and placed it on the table. Kinnear was sitting up, his nose bent grotesquely, blood still dripping from it.

Rawlins said, "Get him outside, Wildew. I'll kill him

11

if he don't get out of here."

Shrugging, Wildew helped Kinnear to his feet. "You hear the man, mister? He aims to kill you if you don't slope out of here."

Kinnear knocked Wildew's hand loose from his arm. He staggered to the door and clutched the jamb. For a moment he held himself there, looking back at Rick, his face bruised and raw. Blood made a red smudge on his upper lip; he raised a hand and wiped his mouth.

Wildew laughed softly. "Looks like a piece of raw beef you're wearing for a face, lawyer."

Turning, Kinnear went out. Wildew moved to the door to watch him, and a moment later the sound of hoof beats came to those in the room.

# CHAPTER 2

### Gunmen Needed

RAWLINS PICKED UP THE CHAIR KINNEAR HAD THROWN at Rick and sat down on it. He said, "Thanks, Rick. No fool like an old fool. I wouldn't have lasted a minute with that hombre."

Wildew came to the couch. He took Rick's right hand and felt of it, closing his fist and opening it, then did the same with his left. He said, "Got any hot water, Nan?"

"I think so," she answered. "There was a good fire in the kitchen when I left."

Rick expected another lecture about fist fighting, but Wildew said nothing until Nan disappeared through the kitchen door. Then he put a hand under Rick's chin and tilting his face up, looked closely at it.

"You ain't got a mark, kid," Wildew said, "except on

12

your chin, and that's just a bruise."

"Butted me like a damned billy goat," Rick said.

Wildew walked to the door and flipped his cigarette stub into the yard. He turned back to Rawlins. "I reckon there's good lawyers and bad lawyers same as in anything else, but I figure Kinnear's a bad one."

"He's more'n bad," Rawlins shouted. "He's a damned lying, ornery son."

"Probably had a horse thief for a father and a sheepherder for a grandfather," Wildew said dryly.

"No he didn't." Rawlins shook his head. "I know his folks. Hard-working farmers. Trouble was they saved their money and starved themselves to send him to school. He came back a lawyer and now he's got the county tucked into the palm of his hand."

Wildew rolled a smoke. He said, "I heard Cord Graham would never have got elected sheriff if he wasn't Kinnear's man."

"You heard right," Rawlins said bitterly.

Nan came in with a pan of hot water and placed it on Rick's lap. Wildew said, "Soak your hands, kid. You may be needing your gun tomorrow. Kinnear left his iron here, but he'll find another one."

Rick put his hands into the water, grimacing with pain. He said, "You had a fire in the stove all right, Nan."

"Won't do no good if it ain't hot." Wildew nodded at Rawlins. "It ain't my way to ask questions of the man I work for, but I am now because me and the kid need to know. What started this ruckus with Kinnear?"

"He accused me of beefing Spargo," Rawlins said. "Claimed he'd throw me into the jug if I didn't make a deal. I jumped him and he knocked me down. Then Rick bought into the fracas."

"What kind of a deal did he want to make?"

The old man pulled at his beard, scowling. Rick, watching him, saw that this was something he didn't want to talk about. It was Nan who prompted him. "They need to know," she said.

"Yeah, maybe they do," Rawlins said. "Well, Kinnear claims Lola Spargo, she's Vance's sister, will be in town on the night stage. Hatchet goes to her. Kinnear says he's gonna marry her. I dunno about that. When she left the valley there was some talk about her wanting to get away from him. Spargo and Kinnear was purty thick. Anyhow, he allowed that if I paid him five thousand dollars, he'd see I didn't have no trouble."

"Hold up," Wildew murmured.

"That's just what it was. Well, I ain't got five thousand dollars. I wouldn't have no truck with a deal like that anyhow."

"Looks like Kinnear aims to go into the ranching business by marrying the Spargo woman," Wildew said.

"That's it," Rawlins agreed, "but everybody knows that Spargo walked big for a gent who was next door to being broke. Prine Tebo holds a mortgage on everything Spargo owned. Lola won't get nothing out of it."

"She will till Tebo takes Hatchet away from her," Wildew said. "You'll be bucking her if you aim to grab Hatchet range."

"She won't bother nobody," Rawlins said. "It's Tebo I've got to see."

Rick knew how it was. Cattle prices had been low for several years. Neither Rawlins nor Jenner had much cash, and their herds were small. It would take money to expand and hold Hatchet range, and Prine Tebo, the Bald Rock banker, was the only man in the county who had that kind of money.

14

Rawlins rose and began pacing the floor. He said, "I didn't kill Spargo. Did you, Matt?"

"No," Wildew answered. "You know I didn't."

"Rick?"

"No," Rick answered.

"Damn it," Wildew said sharply, "anybody who knows me and the kid wouldn't think we done a job like that."

"Sure, sure," Rawlins said impatiently, "but you're both new on this range, and with Cord Graham eating out of Kinnear's hand, it may turn out kind o' rough."

"I figured you'd be paying me and Rick off tomorrow after the burying," Wildew said.

"Didn't plan to. Probably need you more'n ever. Depends on what Tebo says. We'll go to town first thing in the morning and find out what has to be done."

Nan rose. "We're getting along all right, Grandpa. If Kinnear and Lola Spargo want to run Hatchet, let 'em do it."

The old man wheeled to face her. "Not by a damn sight. I've been waiting for this chance. I had Hatchet range once. You know that. I was the first cowman on Pine River. That was way back when the mines around Canyon City was good. I fought Injuns and I organized the Vigilantes to fight rustlers. Then I lost out because times got hard. Had to pull back here with a shirttail-sized herd and three riders, and Spargo moves in. All right. I'm coming back."

"Grandpa, I've got something to tell you. . . ."

"No hurry." Rick got up and set the pan of water on the table. "Plenty of time ahead now."

"Work your hands," Wildew said.

Rick held up his hands, opening and closing them, and Wildew nodded, satisfied. "You're lucky, kid.

15

Awful lucky."

Rawlins stood staring at Nan. "What were you going to tell me?"

Nan glanced at Rick. He shook his head at her, trying to tell her this was not the time. She brought her gaze to her grandfather, saying, "Nothing. It's just that Spargo was trying to push us out of the country. Now he's dead and I don't see no reason for trying to take his place."

"I'm not trying to take his place." Rawlins choked, his face red. "I'm trying to get back the place I used to have. One thing I aim to do before I die is to build the Bent R back to what it used to be. I'll leave you a spread that can be called a spread. When you marry Grant Jenner you ain't going to him empty-handed."

"I won't go to him empty-handed or any other way," the girl cried. "I'll pick my own husband."

Rawlins glared at her, hands shoved into his pockets. He reared back on his tall heels and teetered there, fighting his temper. He said finally, "We'll see. We'll see. I'll talk to Grant in the morning."

"I've thought of something, Lou," Wildew said. "I'm wondering if you have."

"You've thought of what?"

"Take a man like Spargo out of the picture," Wildew said, "and you leave a big hole. Room for a lot to happen. Maybe he was about broke, but he carried a lot of weight, tied up with Kinnear and Cord Graham like he was. Prine Tebo, too, probably. I've seen it happen lots of times. The town boys can't run a ranch, but they like to call the turn because they're making money out of somebody else's hard work."

"What are you driving at?" Rawlins demanded.

"I'm saying they'll pick a winner. Put Hatchet, the Bent R, and the Diamond J together, and they'll have

16

something that'll pay 'em big. This country's always been good. When cattle prices come back it'll be good again. Prine Tebo knows that."

"You mean I ain't big enough to buck 'em?"

"I mean you and Jenner worked together because you had to on account of Spargo. Now suppose the town crowd picks Jenner?"

Rawlins' mouth sagged open, his face showing blank amazement. It was Nan who said, "You're talking loco, Wildew. Even if they picked Grant, he wouldn't play their game. He's Grandpa's friend."

"Sure," Wildew jeered, "and he's in love with you, which same don't prove he wouldn't take their bait if he thought it would make money for him and maybe get his loop on you to boot."

Rawlins threw out a gaunt hand. "I'm paying you to fight, Matt. Don't try to do my thinking for me. I've knowed Grant Jenner since he was a kid."

"Think it over, Lou," Wildew murmured. "Trouble has been my business for a long time, and I've learned one thing. You can't trust nobody when it comes to big money and a pretty girl."

Wildew walked out of the room, Rawlins staring after him and frowning. Rick said, "See you in the morning, Lou." He gave Nan a covert wink and left the house.

Rick walked across the yard, the row of tall poplars to his left making a dark screen against the star-freckled sky. Funny how things worked, he thought. You rode with a man for years. You fought beside him and you slept by the same campfire. You ate out of the same frying pan. With some men you'd know their thoughts and their ambitions; you'd share their dreams and you'd be bound together by the invisible ties of friendship. It was not that way with him and Matt Wildew.

17

He had often wondered why Wildew put up with him. Rick doubted that Wildew understood what the word friendship meant, but he had a certain sense of honor and he possessed a cold-blooded courage that Rick had never seen in another man. Still, Rick did not really know him.

Wildew was sitting on his bunk tugging at a boot when Rick came in. He said, "Sit down, kid. We've got some talking to do."

Rick pulled up a rawhide-bottom chair and sat down. He said, "Fire away," and, drawing the makings from his pocket, rolled a smoke.

"You were a punk kid when I ran into you in Dodge City," Wildew said. "Seventeen. Too young to be smart and old enough to think you were hell on high red wheels. Remember?"

"Sure I remember. You saved my life. I told you once tonight I was beholden to you."

Wildew got his boot off and wiggled his toes. Rick fired his cigarette, mentally recognizing the fact that there had been only one real reason for him sticking to Wildew. At first it had been hero worship. He had thought it was wonderful to be picked up by the great Matt Wildew, but as the years had matured him, he had lost that instinctive sense of awe which had been so overpowering.

In some ways Rick had learned to thoroughly dislike Wildew, although there had never been any hard words between them. Certainly his staying with the gunman had nothing to do with friendship on his part. It boiled down to the fact that Wildew had saved his life. Until he had met Nan, he had not been able to forget that debt.

"It ain't just a case of being beholden," Wildew pulled off his other boot. "Whatever you owed me

18

you've paid. It's a proposition of finding out how smart you are. Sometimes I think you're just stupid. You learned how to tote a gun and how to draw. You learned to shoot straight and you've got guts. It ain't enough."

Rick canted his chair back and put his feet up on a bunk. He said, "I know, Matt. Like using my fists. All right, I'm stupid. I lost my temper tonight. I wasn't packing my gun and when Kinnear knocked the old man down, I jumped in."

"You just jumped in," Wildew mimicked. "That's exactly what I mean when I say you're stupid. You gave Kinnear a hell of a beating, but you left him alive. Now he'll kill you if you don't kill him."

"Then I'll kill him."

"Not if he plugs you in the back, and that's the kind of huckleberry he is. Another thing. This business of falling in love. Hell's bells, Rick, you don't have to love a woman to have one. You can always buy 'em. Then you're done with 'em. You don't owe 'em nothing. Love balls your thinking up, and when a man can't think straight, he's done."

This was like Wildew, Rick thought angrily. A killing machine! Capable of neither love nor friendship. He said irritably, "Quit trying to make me into another Matt Wildew. I ain't built that way."

Wildew leaned back on the bunk, a small smile touching the corners of his mouth. "I found that out a long time ago. You've got a soft streak that's gonna kill you someday." He held up his long-fingered hands and stared at them. "I'm looking to my own future tonight, kid. Sooner or later age does that to a man. The years are one thing I can't lick."

It was the first inkling Rick had ever had that Wildew was considering the fact that age was catching up with

19

him. He thought of the long hours Wildew spent practicing his draw before a mirror, of the great care with which he put on his gun each morning so that the butt hung in exactly the right position, of the inordinate pride which he held in his skill and reputation. If he loved anything, it was his gun.

Wildew dropped his hands. "I didn't really hanker to make that ride to Tucson. I'd rather stay here. I've got a notion that this deal can be made into a big one if we work it right. I mean, big enough to make us a stake. I sure as hell don't aim to be swamping out no saloon when I'm sixty, and I ain't riding for no thirty a month and found."

"I don't savvy. We ain't saved nothing big, I don't see how we can now."

"It ain't a proposition of saving a dollar at a time. We'll get it in a big chunk, providing we don't let this ruckus die. It's my guess Kinnear and the banker have got something big up their sleeves, Kinnear anyhow. He figured on holding Lou up for five thousand. Now he knows damned well Lou didn't have it, so Lou would go to the banker. Maybe he's pulling the same deal with Jenner. That'd get Prine Tebo's hooks into both of 'em."

Rick rubbed out his cigarette. "Lou can't pay us nothing more than he is."

"The big money's on Kinnear's side," Wildew said softly.

Rick looked at him incredulously. "You switching?"

"Maybe. Maybe not. It's worth looking into. Right now I want you to look at yourself. Lou will be done with you the minute you tell him you want to marry the girl. You'll have to switch. You ought to be able to see that."

"I'd never throw in with Kinnear," Rick said hotly.

"Might be other ways to work it. That's something we'll have to figure out. I'm just saying that you're holding a busted straight and there's no sense in putting your money down. Nan said she'd go with you if Lou won't stand for you getting married, didn't she?"

Rick nodded. "She will, too."

Wildew laughed scornfully. "You're crazy as hell, kid. She's got no kin but Lou. She'll stick with him in the windup, and you'll be left high and dry. Now are you going to let your heart flutter like a moon-eyed kid, or are we going after the big dinero?"

Rick walked to the door. He stood staring at the black bulk of the ranch house. There was no light now. Nan and her grandfather had gone to bed, he thought absently, and then his mind returned to Wildew. It didn't add up, the gunman talking this way. It wasn't like him, but Rick had not realized until tonight that Wildew knew he was nearing the end of his string. He was traveling on his reputation, and the time would come when his reputation wasn't enough.

Wildew said, "While you're thinking it over, kid, just remember one thing. In the pinch you can't trust anybody. You've got to look out for number one. Nobody else will."

It was the wrong thing to say. Rick turned, his eyes on Wildew's tough, cynical face. Perhaps the man was right in saying he couldn't trust anybody. That would mean Matt Wildew, too.

"I guess I'll keep on like a moon-eyed kid," Rick said.

"All right." Wildew shrugged and yawned. "I reckon I'll go to bed."

He was as cool as that. Later, with the lamp out, Rick

21

lay on his bunk, listening to Wildew's snores. For the first time in his life he had made a big decision, the kind of decision that would shape all the remaining years of his life. It had been the right one. He was sure of that, yet he was scared. The fear lay like a piece of ice deep in his belly as he considered the future, a future that had no place in it for Matt Wildew.

# CHAPTER 3

### Homecoming

THE SOUTH-BOUND STAGE WHEELED DOWN OUT OF THE timber and took the narrow road cut out of the side of the rimrock above Pine River, hoofs and wheels clattering on the solid rock, the big coach lurching precariously and shaking Lola Spargo with persistent torture. It had been dark for several hours, but the stage had not slackened its speed. Old Billy Cain up there on the high seat had the eyes of an owl, or so they said in Bald Rock. Whether he did or not, he was unquestionably an artist with the silk and the lines.

It had been a long ride from The Dalles, and a tiring one. The dust had drifted in through the windows and covered Lola with a fine film from her little blue bonnet to her slim feet in the high, button shoes; it was in her nose and her mouth and she wondered if she would ever lose the taste of it.

The cliff rose on one side of the road; the canyon dropped away to Lola's right into black nothingness. It was a familiar road to her even though she had not been over it for more than a year. There was a river below her, muddy at this point because of the irrigation west of town, and huge boulders that years of weathering had brought down from the rim. And upstream she could make out the lights of Bald Rock, a scattered few this late at night.

Almost everyone in town would be asleep now. She and Vance used to joke about how the folks in Bald Rock rolled the sidewalks up at nine o'clock. A tame town, a combination cow and farmer town that dozed under the stars and moon by night, and a mild sun by day. Now she had a disturbing feeling that Bald Rock was going to wake up. Her brother's death was enough to wake any town up.

The stage reached the bottom of the canyon and clattered across the plank floor of a bridge and turned upriver toward Bald Rock. The rimrock faded and disappeared into night blackness as the valley widened. On the other side of the river there was a light in a farmer's house, the only light Lola could see, for at this point Bald Rock was hidden from her. The fragrance of cut alfalfa was strong in her nostrils. It was a nice smell, one that she liked and had almost forgotten.

The past year had been a long one. She hated The Dalles where she had worked in a store; she hated the dust and the heat and the wind that howled up the Columbia. She realized more strongly than ever before that this was home, and she would not leave it again, not even for Joe Kinnear who would be waiting for her.

All the way up from The Dalles she had wondered what it would be like now that Vance was dead. Folks would expect her to leave after the funeral. Vance had written what they'd said about her. Thought she was too high-toned for the country. Had to live in a big town. Probably there had been more that Vance hadn't mentioned. He would ignore the gossip that had swept across the valley when she had been a girl. There would be some, she thought with a sudden rush of bitterness, who would remember it whenever her name came up.

There was one other thing Vance had written about. No one could understand, and that included him, why she refused to marry Joe Kinnear. Up and coming, Joe was. He'd be Congressman before they knew it. Governor, maybe. Or Senator. And Joe was not one to let them doubt his future. But they didn't know him. Not the way she did.

She remembered how it had been when she was younger. There was more pleasure in thinking about the earlier years than the later ones. She worshiped Vance. He had been ten years older than she was. Their folks had died when she was twelve. Vance had raised her, along with a housekeeper.

Hatchet hadn't been much of an outfit then. She could remember when Lou Rawlins had been the big man on the Pine River range, big and proddy and tough. Vance had always hated him, and with the help of Joe Kinnear and hard times, Vance had cut Rawlins down to size. Now, she supposed, Rawlins would try to gain back what he had lost.

She thought about how Vance had changed. It was the reason the last few years she had spent on Hatchet had not been pleasant. Kinnear was to blame. Vance had always been greedy and too ambitious. A certain amount of greed and ambition was natural in a man, but the trouble with Vance had been that those qualities had grown out of all proportion until they dictated everything he did.

Vance claimed he held a pat hand. To hell with the small fry. Old Lou had had his day. It was time for a younger man to take hold. With the law looking the

24

other way, and with the bank to strangle life from the small ranchers by withholding credit, Hatchet had moved up the river until it bordered the Bent R and the Diamond J. More than once Lola had said to Vance, "We're big enough. We don't have to keep getting bigger." Then Vance would laugh his big laugh and slap her on the back. "A man never gets big enough," Vance would say. "Before I'm done I'll own half the county and while I'm doing it, I'll help old Joe get to where he wants to go. It's money that makes the mare go and I sure aim to make her go."

Kinnear! Always Kinnear! It had been Joe this and Joe that. She'd gone with him because that was what Vance wanted and she would have done anything for him, anything except marry Joe. That was why she had left. It was easier than having to say No time after time, and then having him urge her with, "But he's big, Sis, and he's gonna be bigger. You couldn't find a better man."

Vance just hadn't understood. She had never been able to make him. He was satisfied with himself, and as far as he was concerned, Joe Kinnear could do nothing wrong. If Vance hadn't changed, if he hadn't become greedier and more belligerent and more threatening, she might have married Joe. She wasn't sure, but she might have. She couldn't ever hate Vance, but she could hate Joe for making Vance what he had become. In that way Joe had been responsible for Vance's death.

The stage was in Bald Rock now. It was nearly midnight, and the only lights along Main Street were in the hotel and the Stag saloon. Billy Cain swung in close to the walk and pulled up in front of the hotel with a violent lurch. Lola's eyes swept the front of the hotel and for a moment she thought Joe was not there. Then

25

Billy Cain stepped down from the high seat, and Kinnear called from the darkness. "Fetch a passenger, Billy?"

"Danged right I did," Billy said. "Purtiest girl in Oregon, so I gave her a ride she'll remember." He opened the door. "Ain't that right, Lola?"

"You certainly did, Billy," she said.

Billy got her valises out of the boot while she stood in the pool of lamplight falling from the hotel lobby across the boardwalk, a tall woman smartly clad in a perfectly fitting gray suit. She could make out Kinnear's big body in the fringe of light. It was not like him to hang back, and she wondered about it.

"You're looking fine, Lola," Kinnear said. "You're prettier than when you left, and I didn't think that was possible."

"Thank you, Joe," she said.

Billy set her heavy valises on the walk beside her. He said, "Funeral's in the morning, ain't it, Joe?"

"That's right," Kinnear answered. "Ten o'clock. We'd have had it today, weather being warm this way, but we held up on your account."

That was like Kinnear. Her year of absence had brought no change in him. He had a way of making it seem that somebody else was to blame if anything went wrong. Like this business of intimating that they would have had the funeral today if she had been home where she belonged.

Billy Cain said, "You're here in time for the funeral. Lola. That's what counts."

"That's right," she said, and picked up her valises.

"I'm sure sorry about Vance," Billy said awkwardly, and because he could not think of anything else to say, he climbed quickly back to the high seat and drove

26

away.

"I'll take your bags, Lola," Kinnear said.

She set them back, preferring to let him have them than to start an argument, and stepped across the walk to the hotel lobby. Glancing back, she saw that Kinnear had picked up her valises and was walking away as if he expected her to follow.

"Joe, I'm staying here," she called.

He turned back, his face indistinct in the shadows. "You're staying with me, Lola. I built a house for you. Remember?"

"I'm staying at the hotel," she said sharply.

"You'll be more comfortable . . ." he began.

Whirling, she crossed the lobby to the desk. The sleepy-eyed clerk stared at her with frank interest. He said, "Evening, Lola. We thought you'd be back for the funeral."

She signed the register, saying nothing to the man. She had become accustomed to this kind of masculine interest before she had left the valley, but now it bothered her. There had always been an element of respect in the way men treated her because she was Vance's sister, but there had been something else, too, something she had not wanted to name that went back to the gossip that had been spread about her when she was a girl.

Tight-lipped, she signed her name and took the key, realizing she was afraid. Now that Vance was dead, the talk would begin again. She started up the stairs, not sure whether Kinnear would bring the valises or not. Vance used to say that Joe was one of the chosen few who had been kissed by destiny, that anything he did turned out right for him, and it was hopeless to hold out against him. Prine Tebo seemed to believe that. So did

27

the sheriff, Cord Graham.

She reached the top of the stairs before she heard Kinnear cross the lobby. She went on along the hall to her room and opened the door before he caught up with her.

"I'll light the lamp." He put the valises down inside her room. "You must have bricks in those bags."

"Gold," she said.

The match flared in his hand and he touched the flame to the wick. He set the chimney into place and turned. "You'll need that gold," he said.

She saw his face distinctly then and she stood rooted there, shocked by surprise. He looked as if a horse had kicked him. One eye was almost closed, his nose was bandaged, one side of his mouth was puffy, and there were a number of cuts and bruises on his chin and cheeks.

"All right," he said testily. "I fell down a well. Let it go at that."

"You must have landed on your face," she said.

"Scraped all the way down," he said, and shut the door.

"I'm tired, Joe. . . ."

He made a savage motion with his hand to silence her. "I know you are. So am I. Tomorrow will be a big day for both of us, but we've got some talking to do."

"Nothing's changed. . . ."

"Damn it," he said harshly, "everything's changed, and you might as well know it. When a man as big as Vance is killed, the whole county's changed."

"We can talk tomorrow, Joe," she cried. "It doesn't have to be tonight."

"Tonight."

He reached for her, the old longing that she had seen

28

so many times in his eyes was there again. She backed away from him. "Don't touch me, Joe. I told you nothing had changed. I meant about you and me."

He dropped his hands to his sides, puzzled as if unable to understand why the woman he loved did not love him. Then anger was in him; his lips tightened and his wide jaw jutted forward the way she remembered it did when he was crossed.

"You'll change your mind, Lola," he said. "It was different when Vance was alive. He shielded you from everything. There's nobody to protect you except me. Seems mighty funny that a woman with your reputation wants to pretend she's hard to get."

She said, "Get out, Joe."

He shook his head. "Not yet. I aim to set you right on a few things. You're thinking you're coming back to a big cattle ranch. You'll just step into Vance's shoes and lord it over everybody. Well, you're wrong, Lola. Hatchet is broke."

She sat down on the edge of the bed, her knees rubber. "I don't believe it."

"Go see Prine Tebo in the morning. He'll tell you. Vance was in debt over his ears. When he was alive, Prine played along because he knew Vance was a good cowman and he'd come out of it. Now it's different. Prine will close you out because he knows damned well you can't run Hatchet. He can't do anything else because he's got his bank to think of."

"You're lying, Joe," she cried. "Nobody ever questioned Vance's financial condition."

"For your sake I wish I was lying," he said. "Vance wanted to be too big too fast. Like I said, Prine played along with him, closing out the little ranchers along the river and selling to Vance. Trouble was Vance didn't

29

have any cash. He gave Prine his notes."

"I'll have time to pay off."

"Not much. Those notes are due this fall." Kinnear shrugged. "Sure, you can move out to Hatchet and stay for a month or two if that will make you any happier."

He stood there looking down at her, a broad-shouldered, formidable man. He went on, "There's one way out. Prine's my friend. I can save Hatchet for you and put in a ramrod in place of Curly Hale who'll run the ranch like Prine wants it run. I want you. You need me. That's fair, isn't it?"

"No. I'll never be so bad off I'll need you."

He pulled up a chair and sat down facing her. "I love you, Lola. Doesn't that mean anything to you?"

"You love yourself, Joe. If you ever wanted me, it was because I was hard to get."

He shook his head. "It's more than that. Sure I love myself, and I'm proud of the record I've made. I didn't start from much, you know, but I'm going a long way. Everybody in Chinook County will tell you the same thing. You don't love me." He spread his hands. "All right, I'll still take you. You want to know why?"

"No. I just want to go to bed."

"Go ahead and undress," he said savagely, "but I'm not leaving until I tell you. I need to be in the cattle business because it will bring me votes. I mean, as the husband of the owner of Hatchet, I'd get votes I'd never get as the district attorney of this county. I'm running for Congress next year. A good-looking wife is a political asset. That's another reason I'll take you on your own terms."

"Go away, Joe," she whispered. "Just go away and let me alone."

"I wanted to talk to you in my home," he said. "I've

30

fixed the house up for you. It's nice, Lola. Nicer than when you saw it. And after I'm elected, you'll go to Washington with me. Isn't that all a woman would want."

"Everything but love, and don't lie about loving me." She stared at him, her hands clenched on her lap. "Joe, I hate you. You must know that."

He rose and kicked the chair across the room in a sudden burst of temper. "Why, damn it, why?"

"Several reasons. One's enough. You killed Vance."

He stood in the middle of the room, motionless, his eyes on her. She saw something in them she had never seen before; it shocked and frightened her. It was more than temper. He moved toward her and stopped a step from the bed, and in that awful moment she knew he was capable of killing her.

"I was Vance's best friend," he said in a low voice. "Why did you say that?"

"I don't know who pulled the trigger, but if it hadn't been for you, he would have been satisfied to have kept Hatchet as it was. Then he wouldn't have been murdered."

"I see," he said, relieved. "Remember one thing, Lola. I had no way of knowing what would happen. I'm sorry he's dead, but I don't regret anything I did for him. I helped him do what he wanted to and he helped me. It was a fair trade."

He began to pace the floor. "None of us knows who killed Vance, although it's my guess Lou Rawlins did it. Cord Graham found Vance's body in the willows beside the river about a mile above the house. He had been shot in the back. No clues, but a thing like that is bound to come out. We'll get the killer and we'll hang him." He stopped and faced her. "But that isn't the question. I'll make it plain. You take me or you'll lose Hatchet."

31

"Then I'll lose Hatchet."

"Just one more thing for you to think about. With Vance gone and you living out there alone, folks will remember something that hasn't been talked about lately."

"I should think," she said angrily, "that a man like you wouldn't want to marry a woman with my reputation."

"I want you. That's reason enough." He laughed hotly. "Anyhow, your reputation won't worry me. I'll make an honest woman out of you."

Without another word he left the room. She rushed to the door and locked it the instant it closed behind him and stood against it, trembling. She had thought she was coming home. Now she wondered if it could ever be home.

She crossed the room and sat down on the bed, thinking of the time she had stayed overnight with one of Hatchet's hands in a line cabin. Nothing had happened. It had been a simple case of necessity, and at the time it had seemed pleasantly exciting. A storm had caught her on Ghost Mountain. She had sought refuge in the cabin and the cowboy had come in after dark. She had stayed because it was a long ways down a rough mountain trail to Hatchet and the storm had kept up until morning.

She'd told Vance about it the next day, laughing because she had taken it lightly, but Vance had been shocked. Crazy, considering the circumstances, but Vance was that way about her, probably because he loved her so much and he had felt responsible because he was all the family she had.

It would have been all right if the cowboy hadn't got drunk the next time he'd gone to Bald Rock and made some brags. Vance had heard it and he'd beaten the man half-dead and made him admit he was lying. The fellow had left the country, but the talk had spread, the tale growing bigger with the spreading.

Nothing had been quite the same after that. Maybe she had imagined it, but it seemed to her that men began looking at her as if wondering what they could have done if they had spent the night in a line cabin with her. It was worse with the women. They wanted to believe the gossip.

The talk had died down in time and been forgotten. Vance was too big to have for an enemy and Kinnear had begun to pay attention to her. He took her to dances and folks began acting as if they were engaged, a rumor that she supposed Kinnear had started. Other men stayed away from her. She blamed that on Kinnear, too.

She undressed and pouring water into the white, blue-rimmed bowl, washed her body, but it seemed to her that the dust had worked through her skin. She put on a nightgown and opened a window, but when she went to bed she could not sleep. A wind came up, banging the blind with monotonous regularity.

It seemed there was no way out. She did not believe that Kinnear had lied about Hatchet's condition. She would see Prine Tebo tomorrow, but she had no real hope that would give her additional time.

She dropped off to sleep and dreamed about her childhood when her folks were alive and Vance was a lanky kid she worshiped. She woke up suddenly, her body tense, remembering the look on Kinnear's battered face when she had said he'd killed Vance. She was shocked by the suspicion that she had been literally right, although at the time she had not meant it that way. She knew then she couldn't quit. She'd play it out to the end.

# CHAPTER 4

## Death of a Dream

RICK WOKE WITH THE INSISTENT BANGING OF THE triangle in his ears. It was Nan's morning announcement that breakfast was ready. He got out of the bunk, his body stiff and sore, and saw that Wildew was gone. It was still early, too early to get up, Rick thought, and he wondered why Nan had got breakfast at this hour.

He dressed quickly, and stepping out into the pale, cold morning, crossed the yard to the back porch. He washed, dried on the roller towel, and went into the kitchen. Rawlins and Wildew were seated at the table; Nan was frying flapjacks. She gave him a quick smile, her back to Rawlins, then her lips formed the words, "I love you."

He started toward her, suddenly reckless, wanting to take her into his arms and defiantly tell old Lou how it was with him. She stood there, waiting, the first early sunlight falling through the window touching her blonde hair with its torch.

Rawlins glanced up, asking, "How do you feel this morning, Rick?"

He said, "Morning, Nan," and stopped a step from her.

The smile faded from her lips and he saw disappointment flow across her face as she turned back to the stove and flipped a flapjack. He went on to the table, angry at himself and uncertain why he had not done what he had wanted to do except that he didn't want this to end. He could not shake off the uneasy

34

feeling that Wildew was right when he'd said that in the windup Nan would stay with her grandfather.

"I asked how you felt," Rawlins said irritably.

"Kind o' stove up." Rick pulled back a chair and sat down. "Like a mule had kicked me in the stomach."

"My jaw hurts where that ornery son cracked me," Rawlins, grumbled. "I'm too old to lose my temper like that. Don't know what got into me."

Wildew glanced impersonally at Rick as if nothing had passed between them. He said, "Wonder how Kinnear's gonna explain his face this morning?"

"We'll be finding out before long," Rawlins said.

Nan brought a platter of flapjacks to the table. Rick helped himself and poured syrup on them, a sense of uneasiness growing in him. He still did not understand Wildew and he didn't know what to expect. Wildew was not given to treachery. That was one of the things Rick admired about the man. If he was going to switch to Kinnear, he'd do it openly and he'd tell Rawlins before he made the switch.

It was plain to Rick now that they had been wrong in thinking the trouble was over. It hadn't started. Rawlins was too stubborn to back down. If he made his play for Hatchet range, he'd need Rick and Wildew more than he had when Spargo was alive and had him backed into a corner. But Wildew was the question mark in Rick's thinking.

There was no more talk until Rawlins and Wildew finished eating and Nan had brought her plate and sat down across from Rick. Then Rawlins, leaning back in his chair, said, "We're stopping at the Diamond J and picking up Grant and his men. Then we'll go to town and see Tebo. I want you boys to go with me. We won't make no threats, but we'll let the old buzzard know that

35

it's my time to howl."

Rick glanced at Wildew, but the man's impassive face told him nothing. He said, "All right, Lou."

Rawlins rose. "Saddle up as soon as you're done, Rick. Hitch up the buggy for me and Nan."

"I'll ride," Nan said.

Rawlins shrugged as if it didn't matter. "I would, too, if my rheumatism wasn't giving me hell."

Funny about the old man, Rick thought. Everything about him was worn out except his spirit. He'd have this last fling at the glory and wealth he had lost; he'd have it or die trying, but he was making two mistakes. One was trusting Wildew, the other was thinking that Grant Jenner had any real core of courage.

"What's this Spargo woman like?" Rick asked.

"Pretty," Nan said.

"You knew her?"

Nan glanced at him as if wondering why he asked. She said, "We weren't friends if that's what you mean. She's older than I am."

"Nan knew her well enough," Rawlins said irritably. "As well as I'd let her. Lola Spargo is a tramp, a damned floozy, and if she hadn't been Vance's sister, she'd have been run out of the valley when she was a girl."

"It was just gossip," Nan said. "Any woman can get herself talked about."

"Not if she behaves," Rawlins snapped. "Done eating, Rick?"

"Sure," Rick said, and rose.

Wildew followed Rick out of the kitchen, neither speaking until they reached the corrals. Then Rick asked, "What are you going to do, Matt?"

Wildew gave him a cool stare. "Change your mind,

36

kid?"

"No."

"Then it ain't none of your damned business what I aim to do."

"Maybe it is."

"No. Not any. I've got one piece of advice. Have it out with Lou today and then get on your horse and drift."

"Why?"

"To save your hide. That's why." Wildew took his rope from the gatepost and walked into the corral. He paused there to look at Rick, a meaningless smile on his lips. "I said you had a soft spot, kid. I don't."

"Meaning what?"

"You never in God's world could pull a gun on me, but I don't have no such handicap."

Rick let it drop there, wondering if Wildew was right. It had never entered his mind before that the day might come when he would have to draw against the gunman, but the thought was there now, worrying him with nagging insistence. Only a hideous prank of fate would make him fight the man who had taught him everything he knew about guncraft. But Wildew was right on one thing. He would not be handicapped by sentiment if it came to a fight.

Later, with the horses saddled and Rawlins' team hitched to his buggy, Rick said, "You've taught me more than just how to pull a gun, Matt. I mean, you've always had some principles."

Amused, Wildew said, "Keep talking, kid. It ain't often I hear about principles."

"Like shooting a man in the back."

Wildew nodded. "I never did, and that includes Vance Spargo. Don't reckon I ever will."

"And about keeping your word."

"I always have."

Nan and Rawlins left the house, Nan wearing her Stetson, leather jacket, and brown riding skirt. Rick watched her cross the yard to them, walking with quick, graceful steps, and he was suddenly angry. He was trapped. No matter how this went, Nan would suffer, and he was the one who would hurt her because she would have to turn against him or her grandfather, the only two men in the world she loved.

"Damn you, Matt," Rick breathed. "You can't switch on the old man like a double-crossing Injun. Nan's going to need some friends."

The enigmatic smile clung to Wildew's lips. "Falling in love clobbers a man's brains. I've told you that often enough."

There was no more time for talk. Rawlins climbed into the buggy and took the lines. Rick helped Nan into the saddle, and as she stepped up, she gave his hand a quick squeeze. Rick and Wildew mounted, and followed Rawlins out of the yard, Nan riding beside the buggy.

The road crossed the river just below the house. The sun was well up, the sky clear except for a few distant clouds that hung above the Cascades to the west. It would be warm again today, Rick thought absently as they swung downriver, the buggy and horses ahead stirring the road dust into a white cloud that hung motionless in the windless air.

The valley was narrow at this point with long fields of hay on both sides of the river. It would have to be cut and stacked within two weeks. That meant hiring a crew of farmers who were always glad to get a few days' work, but if trouble still shadowed the upper valley, they wouldn't come.

It was probably a thought that had not occurred to Rawlins. Or if it had, he was too stubborn to give it due consideration. He might give more thought to it if Prine Tebo turned him down this morning, although Rick wasn't even sure of that. Rawlins would bull it through, win, lose, or draw.

Rawlins swung off the road toward the Diamond J, following a lane that had been fenced off from the hay fields. Jenner had hauled gravel from the river and now he was scattering it in a corral, another chore that needed to be done on the Bent R. Rick remembered how muddy it had been in the spring.

Rawlins called, "Grant," in the peremptory voice he always used to his neighbor.

Jenner leaned his shovel against a corral post and came toward Rawlins, touching his hat to Nan, eyes lingering momentarily on her. He was a chunky man, thirty or more, with a round, pink face that did not tan. He said cheerfully, "Morning, folks," a broad grin on his lips.

"What the hell you working for this morning, Grant?" Rawlins demanded. "You know what day this is?"

Jenner cuffed back his Stetson and scratched his head. "Thursday, ain't it?"

"I don't mean what day of the week," Rawlins shouted. "This is the day they plant Spargo."

Jenner kicked at a rock. "Lou, I didn't figure I'd go to his funeral. Damn it, when a man gives other men the trouble he has, I don't cotton to standing beside his grave and hearing the preacher tell what an amen, righteous son he was."

"I don't, neither," Rawlins snapped, "but I'm going to be in town, and I aim to tell Prine Tebo what we're fixing' to do. Might be we can make a dicker with him."

Jenner chewed his lower lip, eyes again touching Nan's sober face, then he looked at Rawlins. "You want me to go?"

"Sure," Rawlins said as if that were something only a fool would ask. "Get on your horse and buckle on your gun. Where's your boys?"

"At the cow camp," Jenner answered, surprised. "Ain't yours?"

"I mean Fleming and Cardigan. We'll need 'em. We've got to show Tebo we mean business."

"Why, I let 'em go the day Spargo was shot. Hell, Lou, I can't afford a couple of gunslingers. When I hire a man, it'll be one who ain't afraid to get up off his rump long enough to work."

"That so?" Wildew asked softly.

Jenner stiffened. "No offense, friend. Lou can hire all the gunslingers he pleases."

Rawlins' face was stormy. "Grant, I'm surprised at you. We've always worked together. Thought alike. Wanted the same things. Now you turn your fighting men off when we don't know how we stand with Tebo."

"I know how I stand," Jenner said. "I ain't going out looking for a kick in the teeth."

Rawlins threw out a gnarled hand in a wide, inclusive gesture. "Grant, I've dreamed for years about throwing the Bent R and the Diamond J together. You know that. Now I aim to get the papers drawn up today. You coming?"

Again Jenner glanced at Nan's face. Rick, watching closely, wondered what was in the man's mind. He had proposed to Nan so many times and been turned down that he must have known he had no chance with her. But he knew, too, the stubbornness that was in Rawlins. Perhaps he was counting on that to eventually bring Nan to him.

"I'll saddle up," Jenner said.

"Wait," Nan said, her voice low. "I'll make one thing clear to both of you. You can bargain over cows and horses, but you won't bargain over me."

"I never intended to," Jenner said. "If Lou wants me to throw in with him, I ain't kicking."

Nan reined her horse around, calling, "Rick, come on. Let them haggle."

Rawlins reared up in his seat, bawling, "Nan, you ain't in no hurry."

She didn't stop. Rick followed her, catching the grin on Wildew's face as he rode away. "You're holding a busted straight," the gunman had said, and now he might have added that Rick was even more stupid than he had thought.

Rick did not catch Nan until they were in the road, and when he came up alongside her, she flung at him, "We waited, Rick. Now see what it got us."

"Nothing that it ain't got us before," he said, "or won't get us later."

Her face softened. "I guess that's right, but I feel sorry for Grant, being dragged into a crazy deal he doesn't want. He's let Grandpa lead him around by the nose so long it's got to be a habit."

Rick said nothing to that. He stared ahead at the road which followed the south bank of the river, wondering why he could not shake off the feeling that Wildew was right when he'd said Nan would stick to her grandfather in the pinch. Probably Wildew was right, too, in saying that being in love clobbered a man's brains.

Wildew thought about Nan in the cold, logical way he thought about everything. It was not possible for Rick to think about her that way. He wanted Nan to go with him

41

when he left the Bent R, wanted it so much that he could not bring himself to consider the possibility of losing her.

He glanced at Nan who was now strangely preoccupied and seemed unaware of his presence beside her. She was young, not much over eighteen, and Rick knew from what she had said that she had never thought seriously about any other man except Grant Jenner. Even before she had been old enough to consider marriage, Lou Rawlins had started talking about Jenner being the right man for her.

The regular Bent R hands were older men who had worked for Rawlins as long as Nan could remember. It came to Rick now that he was probably the first young, single man who had been on the ranch since Nan had grown up. Perhaps she had used him to declare her independence; perhaps it was the reason she had wanted to tell Rawlins about being in love with him.

Nan's saying she felt sorry for Jenner troubled Rick. If Rawlins quit trying to force him or her, she might think differently about him. It seemed to Rick that she was too violent in her insistence that she disliked Jenner. Doubt began to plague him now for the first time since he had kissed her that day on the rim.

Impulsively, Rick said, "We'll have it out with Lou tonight."

She glanced at him, frowning. "All right, Rick."

The smile that came so easily to her lips was not there. She turned her eyes away from him again to stare ahead. He had never seen her buried as deeply in her thoughts as she was now, and he could not help wondering if she was thinking about Jenner.

They passed several deserted ranches that belonged to Hatchet, places Prine Tebo had closed out and sold to

Spargo. Windows were broken, doors hanging from a single hinge, yards grown up with weeds. People had lived here; they had worked here and dreamed their dreams, and they had lost.

Thinking about it now, it struck Rick that Spargo's, death had not really changed anything. Lou Rawlins was fooling himself in believing that it did. If Tebo wanted to, he'd take Hatchet, lock, stock, and barrel, and he'd pick his own men to run it. If Rawlins kept on with the crazy idea he had, he'd go broke and he'd drag Jenner down with him. It was crazy because he was independent of Tebo now. If he was smart, he'd let well enough alone.

There was no use for Rick to tell Rawlins where he was headed. The old man would flare up and say he was paying Rick to fight and not to think. It was true, a fact which did not make Rawlins any less the fool for making this last, futile grab for glory.

They passed Hatchet three miles above town. It lay a short distance from the road, the buildings surrounded by hay fields, rimrock rising directly behind them. Rick had never been in the house, a two-story frame structure that was painted white, but he had heard that Vance Spargo had furnished it well. The barns were big, the corrals forming a labyrinth to the west.

The talk was that cattle prices were on the up grade again. If Spargo had lived, he could have cleared himself with the bank. It was strange that he had been killed just now, and it struck Rick that the murder had been timed right for the banker. He frowned, considering the possibility that Tebo had been responsible for the killing, and decided against it. Like Grant Jenner, Tebo did not seem to be the kind.

"Think you'll enjoy running the big house?" Rick

43

asked.

"What ever made you ask that?"

"Lou wants to put you there."

She shrugged. "He won't. We might as well be reasonable, Rick. We both know what Tebo will say."

"Lou's gone loco about this whole thing," Rick said. "He's counting on Matt and that's wrong. Likewise he's counting on Jenner and that's another mistake."

"You tell him, Rick," Nan said, her voice curt.

"He won't believe me."

"He wouldn't believe me, either." She sighed, her face shadowed by worry. "I wish I could change him, but he's never listened to anyone else and he won't start now."

Again they rode in silence. The nagging doubts that had begun to plague him made him wonder if she really loved him. Even if she did he doubted if she really understood the decision she must make tonight. If she went with him, she left her grandfather to be defeated and broken alone. If she stayed she would give Rick up. There could be no middle ground.

It was after nine when they reached town. They reined up in front of the Mercantile, Nan saying, "I'm going to buy a dress. Take my horse to the stable, will you?"

He nodded. "What'll I tell Lou?"

"Tell him I'm spending the day with Mary Dolan."

She stepped down and Rick rode on along the street to the stable, leading her horse. Mary Dolan was Nan's best friend and they always visited when Nan came to town. They'd spend the afternoon working on the dress. Rawlins wouldn't like it because he'd want Nan to go to the bank with him, but it was one decision which he would have to accept.

Leaving the horses in the stable, Rick walked back up the street to the bank. There was a black bow on the door, and a notice that read: CLOSED UNTIL NOON FOR VANCE SPARGO'S FUNERAL. Rawlins wouldn't like this, either, Rick thought, and waited there on the walk until the old man arrived, Wildew and Jenner flanking his buggy.

Rawlins pulled up in front of the bank and stepped down. He asked brusquely, "Where's Nan?"

"Buying some goods in the store. She's going to spend the day with Mary Dolan."

"The hell." Irritated, Rawlins pulled at his beard, glanced at the store, and then shrugged. "Well, they'll be up to their necks in pins and needles and thread till dark."

"The bank's closed for the funeral," Rick said.

Rawlins glanced at the door, then jerked his watch out of his pocket and looked at it. "Ain't time for the funeral yet. Prine's in the back room, chances are." He jerked his head at Jenner and Wildew who had dismounted and tied. "Come on. You, too, Rick."

Rawlins strode around the corner of the bank to the side door and tried the knob. The door was locked. He moved to the window and looked in. "Yeah, he's there." He tapped on the glass, shouting, "Open up, Prine," and stepped back to the door.

The lock turned and the door opened. Tebo poked his head out, saying, "Sorry, Lou. I'll be open after dinner."

Rawlins said, "You're open now," and putting a shoulder against the door, shoved Tebo back and walked in.

The banker was a slight, medium-tall man about Rawlins' age with a carefully trimmed white mustache and a pair of piercing black eyes that age had not dulled.

Now they reflected the rising anger in him. He said, "You're riding high today, Lou."

Tebo stepped back to his desk and stood dourly staring at Rawlins. His office was not a large room, and when Rick, Wildew and Jenner pushed in behind Rawlins, it seemed crowded. Rawlins moved forward so that the desk was between him and the banker, his gaunt frame straight, bony shoulders back.

"Prine, me and Grant are throwing our ranches together. We're taking over Hatchet range."

"I expected that." Tebo's thin lips formed a tight line across his pale-skinned face. "Forget it. The land along the river is deeded and belonged to Vance. It'll go to Lola now."

"I'll buy it."

"What with?"

"I want a loan. Spargo just held the title. You could have taken it over any time you wanted to. I'm asking for a big enough loan to buy Hatchet's herd. You're no cowman, Prine."

Tebo raised a hand and scratched his smoothly-shaven chin, eyes moving around the half-circle of men who faced him and came back to Rawlins. "This a threat?"

"Call it that if you want to. I'm just telling you we're moving onto Hatchet range. I'm coming back, Prine, all the way."

"You'll never come back," Tebo snapped. "I'm not forgetting how it was, but what's past is past. Stay where you are."

"Damn it," Rawlins bawled, "if I have to draw a picture for you, I'll draw it."

"No need to." Tebo glanced at the clock on the wall, then picked up his hat. "Time for the funeral."

46

"Do I get that loan?" Rawlins demanded. "Me and Grant, I mean?"

"No," Tebo said curtly, and walked out of the office into the morning sunlight.

# CHAPTER 5

## Suspicion

RICK, WATCHING RAWLINS' FACE, THOUGHT THAT IT was hell to be old. It was bad enough for a young man to see his dreams blow up before his eyes, but a young man had time to dream again. Lou Rawlins didn't. Now he seemed years older than he was; his shoulders sagged as if he lacked the strength to hold them erect.

"We're all right as long as that old buzzard ain't got his hooks into us," Jenner said. "Let's go home and forget it."

Rawlins acted as if he hadn't heard. He stumbled out of the office and went on around the corner of the building to Main Street. He stood on the corner a moment, watching Tebo until he disappeared into the church. Rick, standing behind the old man, could hear the organ that had just begun to play.

Jenner laid a hand on Rawlins' arm, his cherubic face very grave. He said, "Let's go back home, Lou. No use bucking a stacked deck. It's Kinnear and Cord Graham, too. We both know how it is."

Strength seemed to flow back into Rawlins. His shoulders were erect now, and as he rolled a cigarette, his fingers were steady. "A few years ago I could have walked into that bank and got any amount of money I wanted. Well, I'll get it yet, Grant. I went at this

47

wrong."

"It's no use," Jenner said.

Wildew glanced at Rick, his face expressionless, and Rick felt irritation stir in him. A stake, the gunman had said, a big stake. He was like a cat waiting for the fattest mouse in the nest to come by. Rick moved up to stand beside Rawlins. He said, "Jenner's right, Lou."

Rawlins reared back, scowling. "You quitting?"

"No, but . . ."

"You've had your pay at the first of every month," Rawlins said ominously. "I still need your gun, and I need Matt's. If you and Matt are backing out, I want to know it. Now."

"Not me," Wildew murmured.

"I'll string along," Rick said, "but I'll do my own thinking."

It seemed to satisfy Rawlins. He fired his cigarette, nodding at Jenner. "I wish you hadn't let Cardigan and Fleming go. Reckon they're still in town?"

"Dunno," Jenner answered.

"Maybe they're in the Stag. Let's go get a drink."

Rawlins stalked across the dust strip to the saloon, Jenner beside him. The Diamond J man didn't like it, Rick thought, but habit would keep him in line for a while, habit and the hope that by siding Rawlins, he could make Nan love him. Perhaps he could, Rick thought. Then he wondered why after all these weeks he had begun to doubt Nan's love when he had been so sure of it only a few hours before.

Rick waited until Rawlins and Jenner were across the street, then he followed reluctantly. He had neither respect nor trust in Fleming and Cardigan. Wildew, too, had lingered behind. Now he fell into step with Rick, saying, "So now you're going to do your own thinking."

"You've always done yours," Rick said.

"Sure," Wildew murmured. "I've already done my thinking on this whole business, and that old fool would sure be surprised if he knew what my thinking was."

Rick pushed through the batwings. Rawlins and Jenner were at the bar, and Rick saw that Horseface Fleming and Deke Cardigan were here, playing poker at a back table. They were a queer team, Fleming big and ugly with a long, broad-nosed face that gave him his name, Cardigan small and fine-featured and soft of voice.

Rawlins motioned toward Fleming and Cardigan who came to the bar. No one else was in the saloon but the bartender. Rawlins said, "Whiskey." He looked at Rick and Wildew who had paused just inside the batwings, and in a sudden burst of temper, shouted at them, "Come on, come on. We're drinking."

Rick glanced questioningly at Wildew. One of the first things that Wildew had pounded into Rick was the fact that a gunman must choose between his trade and whiskey.

"If you want to slow up and get to seeing double, whiskey is the surest way to do it," Wildew often said. But this called for at least a beer. Wildew nodded, and they moved to the bar.

"Beer," Wildew said.

"The same," Rick said.

Rawlins shot them a scornful glance, then he swung to face Fleming. "You boys got anything on the string?"

The big man grinned. He was the talker, but Rick had always considered Cardigan the more dangerous man. He and Wildew had run across Fleming and Cardigan several times during the last six years, but their meetings had been casual.

49

Neither Fleming nor Cardigan would be above shooting a man in the back, Rick thought. Now, glancing at Jenner's somber face, it seemed to him that the Diamond J man was not the kind who would order a killing, but it was a probability that proved nothing in a situation like this. Fleming and Cardigan were not particular who they worked for, and there were other men besides Jenner who might have wanted Vance Spargo dead.

"Well, can you talk?" Rawlins demanded in his short-tempered way.

"Never saw the day I couldn't talk." Fleming helped himself to a drink. "I was just thinking, Lou. How about it, Deke? Have we got anything on the string?"

"Nothing good," Cardigan said.

"Grant's taking you back," Rawlins said.

Fleming's bushy brows lifted in surprise. "Now that's funny. Real funny. You see, Grant told us purty damned plain that a man who drew our kind of money had better do some work. He even mentioned pitchforks." He looked down at his big hands. "We can't afford nothing like that. A pitchfork tightens up a man's muscles."

"The old job," Rawlins snapped. "We need you two, me and Grant."

Fleming pinned mocking eyes on Jenner. "That you talking, Jenner? Or just your future pappy-in-law?"

Rick stood at the end of the line. He stepped back from the bar, temper pulled to the breaking point. He felt at odds with everybody. Now he could focus his anger on Fleming. He would be doing Rawlins a favor, he thought, if he could break this deal up now.

"Let's have it, Horseface," Rick said, powder-gray eyes fixed on Fleming's ugly face. "You want the job or not?"

50

Fleming looked past Rawlins at Rick, his tough, wild face suddenly alive with interest. "It's the kid, Deke, talking up like a man."

"He is a man," Rawlins snapped. "You seen Kinnear's face today?"

"Yeah. Said he fell down a well. The kid do it?"

"He done it," Rawlins answered.

Fleming shrugged meaty shoulders. "Kinnear's one gent. I'm another. Now I never like to be prodded. . . ."

"The kid's right." Wildew moved in front of Rick. "I don't figure we need you two. That ain't my sayso, but one thing's sure. If you don't want the job, make it plain."

Fleming licked dry lips. Rick had seen this same thing happen many times. Even Horseface Fleming who never for a moment doubted his own toughness wanted no trouble with Matt Wildew.

"Why sure, Matt," Fleming said. "What do you say, Deke? We going back to the Diamond J?"

"No," Cardigan said in his soft voice. "We can do better."

"That's what I figure," Fleming said loudly, and stalked back to the table where he had been playing cards, Cardigan following.

"Why, that smart-aleck son of a. . ." Rawlins began.

"Oh hell," Jenner said wearily. "Let's play a few hands, Lou."

Jenner picked up a bottle and glasses and moved to a table. Rawlins hesitated, glaring at Fleming and Cardigan, then called to the barman, "Fetch us a new deck, Applejack." He nodded at Wildew. "Want to sit in?"

"Might as well," Wildew said.

Rick shook his head at Rawlins and moved to a

51

window. The funeral procession was in the street, a black hearse leading it. The bartender took the cards to Rawlins and came to stand beside Rick.

"Everybody in town but me went to the funeral," Applejack said in a sulky tone. "Here I am, waiting on a has been and a bunch of gunslingers."

"Not Jenner," Rick said.

Applejack snorted. "Nobody counts him."

"Why didn't you go?"

"Kinnear," Applejack said bitterly. "He's a hell of a man to work for. Should have locked up same as the bank and everything else, but not Kinnear."

Rick had not known before that Kinnear owned the Stag, and it struck him as being queer that the lawyer had not closed the saloon, considering the fact that he was supposed to have been Spargo's closest friend. He said, "Funny he didn't lock up."

"It ain't funny," Applejack muttered. "Ain't funny at all. Big man, Joe is. Got big by doing tricks like this. He nurses every dollar he gets his hands on till it hatches another one."

The hack that followed the hearse was directly in front of the saloon now. Kinnear was driving, a tall, handsome woman in a black dress beside him. Prine Tebo rode in the seat behind them.

"Who is she?" Rick asked.

"Lola Spargo. Vance's sister."

Other rigs wheeled by, townsmen and farmers from below town, and the Hatchet crew on horses, the ramrod, Curly Hale, in the lead. With a bitter oath, Applejack yanked off his apron and threw it on the bar.

"I'm going," he said. "I don't give a damn if Kinnear fires me. Vance was a friend of mine."

He put on his coat and left the saloon. Rick went

52

outside and dropped down on the long bench, shadowed by the wooden awning. He rolled a cigarette and fired it; he took a few puffs and threw it into the street, finding the taste bitter to his tongue.

He was not sure why the dark mood was on him. Perhaps it was because of what Wildew had said the night before, and he resented the way Wildew had stepped between him and Fleming. It had happened before and he had taken no offense. Wildew often said that there was no sense in having trouble unless you were paid for it, and he did have a talent for stopping trouble before it started. But this seemed different. He and Wildew owed nothing to each other now.

Time dragged out for Rick. He began to whittle on the bench that already held half a season's carvings on it and would be nearly whittled up by the time cold weather came. He thought absently that Bald Rock, its Main Street now devoid of human life except for him, was little different from a hundred towns where he and Wildew had tarried.

Dobes in the southwest, frame buildings here in the north. Or long ones. But essentially everything was the same. Horses standing hip-shot in the sun. Dogs dozing in the street dust. And always there was trouble or the promise of trouble. Wildew could smell it miles away.

He was tired of it, tired of Wildew, tired of everything he had learned about this business. It was not Rick Malone's life, and he felt a keen regret for the wasted years. He knew now he had been growing tired of it for a long time. It had taken Nan to wake him up, to show him that life held the promise of a great many things he would never find if he stayed with Wildew.

The grave-side ceremony was over. Rigs were streaming back, talk flowed along the street, and the dogs fled to the relative safety of the alleys. The hearse passed and turned off Main Street. The Hatchet crew rode by, somber-faced. Then Rick saw Kinnear's rig pull to a stop; Prine Tebo stepped down and held a hand up to assist Lola Spargo.

Rick saw Lola's face clearly now. She had been weeping. That was to be expected, but there was more than that, a genuine sadness that went deeper than the sorrow she must have felt for her brother. She had loved him, Rick thought, deeply and devotedly, and for some reason the knowledge shocked him.

He had mentally placed Spargo and Kinnear in the same pigeonhole of life, but there must have been some good in Vance Spargo if a woman like Lola could love him. Spargo and Kinnear, then, must not have been alike, for Rick was convinced that there was little if any good in Joe Kinnear.

For a moment Lola and Tebo stood on the walk talking to Kinnear. Applejack strode past Rick and pushed through the batwings, his mouth hard set. Other men drifted by and some went into the saloon, and then Rick was aware that Fleming and Cardigan had come out of the Stag and were standing on the boardwalk, idly watching the sudden burst of activity.

Rick paid no attention to Fleming and Cardigan. His eyes were on Kinnear's bruised face, and he saw with satisfaction that the man's nose had been set and bandaged, that a corner of his mouth was still puffy and one eye half-closed.

Kinnear nodded as if in agreement with something Tebo had said, and turning his team, drove back up the street toward the cemetery. Tebo talked to Lola a moment, then he swung away to the bank, and Lola came along the boardwalk, toward the hotel.

Lola was staring directly ahead of her, seeing no one. Her mind, Rick thought, was on the funeral and her brother, and he wondered what she would try to do with Hatchet. If anybody was trying to bluff with nothing better than a busted straight, it was Lola Spargo.

She passed Rick, unaware of his gaze, and had gone on beyond Fleming and Cardigan when Fleming's words, loud enough for Lola to hear, came clearly to Rick's ears, "There goes my kind of woman, Deke. They say a man can sleep with her for the asking."

Rick came up off the bench in a lunge; he grabbed the collar of Fleming's coat back of the neck with his left hand and the slack seat of Fleming's pants with his right and swung the big man off his feet. Rick couldn't have done it if Fleming had not been taken completely by surprise. As it was, he had Fleming in the air and across the walk to the horse trough in front of the Stag before the man began to kick and bawl like a bull calf under a hot iron.

"Drop him, Malone," Cardigan called.

Rick didn't look back. He slammed Fleming onto the ground beside the trough. The man fell flat, spraddled out, and gave another bawl of humiliation and rage. He got to his hands and knees and Rick hit him across the back of the neck with a brutal, downswinging blow that struck with the power of a descending pick handle. Fleming went back down into the dust, almost knocked out by the blow.

Rick lifted Fleming, holding him by the coat collar and the seat of the pants as he had before. This time Fleming had little capacity for resistance. Rick shoved his head into the slimy water that filled the horse trough and held it there.

A crowd had gathered, some of the men yelling for

55

Rick to drown Fleming. Rick didn't know how many had heard what Fleming had said, but it was evident that he had few friends in the crowd. Rick yanked Fleming's head out of the water and shook him.

"Swallow what you said, Fleming," Rick said. "Tell 'em you're the damnedest liar in Chinook County, or I'll drown you as sure as there ain't no drinking water in hell."

"Lemme go," Fleming choked. "Lemme get my gun and, I'll . . ."

His head went back into the water. This time Rick held it, bubbles coming up around Fleming's ears, big body bucking and twisting in Rick's grip. Then Cord Graham was beside Rick, a gun rammed into his back.

"Trying to drown a man, Malone?" the sheriff demanded.

Lou Rawlins was on the other side of Rick, shaking his arm. "Quit it, you fool. You ain't no good if they hang you."

Reason returned to Rick's mind. He pulled Fleming back from the trough and slammed him onto his back. Water sloshed from his head and shoulders and trickled away through the dust.

"You made one mistake, Sheriff." Rick jabbed a finger at Fleming who lay motionless as he fought for breath, his eyes glassy. "He ain't a man."

"You're right about that," Graham admitted. "Fact is, we could do without the collection of polecats and coyotes that Lou and Grant fetched into this county last spring, and that includes you."

"Now maybe you could," Rick said.

Graham dug a toe into Fleming's ribs. "You take this up with your cutter, mister, and I'll have you both in the jug." He wheeled to Rawlins. "I want to see you and

56

Grant in my office. Fetch Wildew and Malone along."

Graham strode away. Jenner, standing behind Rawlins, said in a low tone, "That took guts, Malone. I heard Fleming. You made some friends today."

"And some enemies," Wildew murmured.

Wildew had his right hand wrapped around gun butt, eyes on Deke Cardigan. It was not until then that Rick remembered Cardigan had ordered him to let Fleming go. It was Wildew who had kept Cardigan out of it.

"Thanks, Matt," Rick said. "I didn't expect it."

"Come on," Rawlins said irritably. "Let's see what the star toter wants."

Rawlins pushed through the circle of men, Jenner behind him. Wildew said, "He wanted us, too, Rick."

"Sure, sure," Rick said, and walked to where Cardigan stood, hate a naked and vicious thing in his eyes. "Any time you want to take this up, Deke, it'll be all right with me."

"I'll take it up," Cardigan said in his soft voice. "Don't make no mistake about it."

Rick went on toward the jail, the crowd breaking away to let him through, Wildew keeping step with him. When they were almost to the jail, the gunman murmured, "I made a mistake calling you stupid, kid. You ain't smart enough to be stupid."

Rick said, "We ain't fooling each other, Matt. How come you put the hobbles on Cardigan?"

The enigmatic smile curled the corners of the gunman's mouth. "Habit, kid. But remember what I told you before. You've got a soft spot that'll kill you."

"I still wouldn't swap places with you," Rick said, and went into the sheriff's office.

It was a small room in the front of the building that was mostly county jail. There was a desk and a few rawhide-bottom chairs and a gun rack beside the door that led into the corridor which ran between the cells. Graham stood at his desk, long fingers tapping its spur-scarred top. He belonged to Rawlins' and Tebo's generation, a raw-boned man with a sweeping gray mustache, the portion above his mouth stained brown by tobacco.

There was much of the early history of Chinook County that Rick had never heard, but he did know that Rawlins, Tebo, and Graham had known each other in the early days and had been among the first settlers. At one time Graham had been a cowhand on the Bent R when Rawlins had been the big man on Pine River and Tebo had been a struggling storekeeper, his stock a barrel of whiskey, a few bolts of cloth, and some groceries.

Now just the three of them were left from the dozens of settlers who had come to Chinook County when it had been a part of Wasco County almost two generations before, and their relative positions had been reversed. Staring at Graham's craggy face, it occurred to Rick that this change had a good deal to do with the hopeless urge to regain his lost wealth and prestige that constantly prodded Lou Rawlins.

"This won't take long," Graham said. "I'll give it to you straight. Vance Spargo was a friend of mine, which makes more reason for me to find his killer than the fact that I'm packing the star. I'll find him and I'll hang him."

"If you're thinking any of us did it . . ." Jenner began.

"That's just what I'm thinking," Graham snapped. "Not you, Grant. You're a mite weak in the gizzard. That brings me to you, Lou."

Rawlins swelled like an infuriated game cock.

"You're a fool, Cord, a blasted, lame-brained fool, and you'd never have got to where you have if Joe Kinnear hadn't picked you up and shoved you into the office by the nape of your neck."

Graham's face reddened. "I'll let that go for now, Lou. I've been over the place where Vance was killed and I ain't picked up a clue of any kind, but one thing seems purty dear. There wasn't no fight. Vance had been talking to his killer, I'd say, judging by their tracks, then he made the mistake of turning his back and he got it between the shoulder blades."

"You're a little slow taking this up," Wildew said softly.

"I didn't figure the killer was going anywhere," Graham said. "He must have been somebody Vance knowed. Maybe a friend. Or a man Vance wasn't afraid of. Maybe somebody he didn't figure had the guts to do it. Otherwise he wouldn't have turned his back."

"A friend," Rick said. "Ever think of Kinnear?"

Graham gave him a scornful look. "That's the craziest thing I've heard yet. Joe was his best friend and he's in love with Vance's sister. Besides, he's the district attorney."

"There's Prine Tebo," Rick said. "And you."

"And his foreman, Curly Hale," Graham snorted. "Look, Malone. There was a time in this valley when men got beefed over nothing much. Some name-calling, maybe. Or a poker quarrel. Well, that day's gone. It takes a damned good reason nowadays to kill a man, and Lou's the only one I can think of who's got it."

It was a good point, Rick knew, and one that could not be discounted, although there was some doubt in his mind about Rawlins being the only one in the valley who had reason to kill Spargo. There were others who

59

had suffered from Hatchet's expansion. He glanced at the red-faced Rawlins, and he began to wonder. The old man might have done it.

"Arrest me if that's what you're getting around to," Rawlins said sullenly, "but even a chuckle-headed idiot like you would know I wouldn't plug a man in the back."

"Not if you was the old Lou Rawlins I used to know," Graham said, "but you ain't. You've had some bad luck and it's made you loco."

"Arrest me," Rawlins repeated. "See if you can get a conviction."

Graham shook his head. "Not today. I just wanted you to know you're under suspicion."

"Why are you telling him?" Rick asked.

"He'll give himself away," Graham said. "I'm just waiting till he does."

"Maybe if Lou decided not to make a try for Hatchet range," Rick said, "you wouldn't be so suspicious."

"What's that got to do with it?" Graham demanded. Then, before Rick could answer, he hurried on, "It adds up pretty good, Lou talking to Prine like he done, and wanting to move in on Hatchet."

"It adds up that way because you're doing the figuring. There's something that maybe you don't know about Kinnear. He came out to the Bent R last night and told Lou that if he'd dig up five thousand, he wouldn't have no trouble over Spargo's killing."

"Hogwash," Graham snapped. "Anybody else hear that proposition?"

"No."

Graham laughed shortly. "All right. Forget it."

"How about you, Jenner?" Rick asked. "Did Kinnear make that offer to you?"

Jenner hesitated, uneasy eyes touching Rick's face and turning away. "Yeah," he answered. "The same deal."

"Now figure it out, Sheriff," Rick said. "Kinnear wants Hatchet to have the valley from here on up to the head of the river. Or maybe it's Tebo who wants it. Same thing. Now if Jenner and Lou got boogered into raising that five thousand, they'd have to mortgage their spreads to the bank. Then Tebo and Kinnear would have 'em where they want 'em."

"More hogwash," Graham snapped. "Takes more'n that kind of talk to smear honest men."

"I ain't been in the valley long," Rick went on, "but a man don't need to be here long to see how you and Tebo and Kinnear are hooked up. It's my guess that Spargo kicked over the traces about something and one of you three plugged him."

It seemed to Rick that he had hit dead center. Graham's face lost its color. He dug a plug of tobacco out of his pocket and bit off a chew with a savage twist. Then, making a show of his anger, he said, "I told you that talk won't get you nowhere." He nodded at Rawlins. "That's all,Lou. I told you I just wanted you to know."

"It's not quite all."

They turned to the door. Lola Spargo stood there, tall and straight-backed, her head held high. Graham, taken by surprise, stammered, "This ain't none of your affair, Lola."

"You're wrong, Cord," she said evenly. "I've been listening to some of the talk, and I think Mr. Malone came nearer to the truth than he knew. Naturally I'm interested in seeing that my brother's murderer is caught and punished."

61

"He will be," Graham muttered.

"I came here for something else." Lola pinned her eyes on Rawlins. "I will not apologize for the wrong things Vance did, and I never heard of you apologizing for the things you did when you were so high and mighty you didn't have to answer to anyone. The future is something else. Mr. Tebo told me you intend to take Hatchet range. Don't try it, Rawlins, unless you want to bathe this valley in blood."

Whirling, Lola walked away, the staccato crack of her heels on the boardwalk slowly fading. Rawlins rubbed a hand across his face, bitter old eyes on Graham. He said, "You ain't big enough for this job, Cord. Not unless you get up off your knees."

Rawlins stomped out, the others following, Graham glowering at their backs. Wildew said softly, "You handled that pretty well, kid, but do you know what you done?"

"I made another enemy," Rick said.

"That you did. And what color do you like for a coffin?"

"I don't give a damn."

Rawlins called over his shoulder, "Let's put that feed bag on. Then we'll go see Prine again."

Rick and Wildew fell into step behind Rawlins and Jenner. Glancing sideways at Wildew's tough, knife-edge face, it struck Rick that he might be able to figure out what Kinnear and Tebo and Graham would do. Lou Rawlins and Grant Jenner would run true to form, but there would be no outguessing Matt Wildew.

If it were not for Nan, Rick would get his horse and ride out of Pine Valley. It was nothing to him what happened to Rawlins or Jenner or the rest. Nothing at all, and he would be glad to be out of it. But there was

62

Nan. For the first time in his life he was bound by a tie he could not break, not until she made her decision tonight.

# CHAPTER 6

## Among Needles and Pins

IT WAS AFTER TEN WHEN NAN DECIDED ON A PIECE OF flowered organdie. She had it cut and wrapped, and asked the storekeeper to charge it. He hesitated, scratching the sharp tip of his nose, and for a moment she thought he was going to refuse.

She could not have blamed him if he had, for she knew how large the bill had become that her grandfather owed and it was doubtful if he would pay this fall. He had borrowed money from Tebo to pay gunmen's wages to Rick and Wildew, and he would keep on paying them, even now that the need was past. The storeman would be thinking that if Lou could afford to hire gunhands, he could pay a bill that was long overdue.

The storekeeper said, "All right, Nan," and wrote it down.

She walked out into the sharp sunlight, blinking a moment after being accustomed to the gloom of the store, and walked around the corner to Mary Dolan's house. She hadn't really needed the dress. It had been months since she had gone to a dance. Rick had never taken her to one and it was not probable he would now.

She had just wanted it. She could show off to Rick even if no one else saw it. She would work on it with Mary, and it might make the talking easier. She had to talk. She had to, and Mary was the only one who would understand.

Nan heard the organ before she reached Mary's house and knew that the funeral was started. The church was less than a block away, the door and windows open, and as she knocked on Mary's front door, the sound of the soprano voice of the preacher's wife singing "Sweet By and By" came clearly to her.

Mary was working in her sewing room. Nan could hear her machine. She rapped again, louder, glancing at the tall letters on the window beside the door: DRESSES MADE TO ORDER. She hoped that Mary wasn't tied up with an order from Mrs. Tebo. The banker's wife had kept Mary alive since she had moved to town and she could not afford to turn her down if one of her rush jobs had come in.

The machine stopped and Nan heard Mary's steps in the hall. The door opened. Mary cried, "Nan, I've been wondering what had happened to you," and her smile was quick and genuine.

Mary Dolan was three years older than Nan, a fully matured woman who was too big in hips and breasts and just a little dowdy. She had lost all interest in men, for her husband had died the year before, and her grief was still as poignant as it was the day he had been buried.

"I couldn't stay away any longer." Nan motioned toward the church. "They've started."

Mary's smile fled from her lips, leaving it bitter. "I'm probably the only person in town who isn't there. Maybe I should go and dance on his coffin. That would give the old hens something to talk about, wouldn't it?"

"They've got enough now," Nan said, "and they'll have more."

She went in, Mary closing the door. Of all the people who had lost their homes along the river to Hatchet, only Mary was left in the valley. The others had gone away to try again somewhere else, but Mary possessed a stubborn streak that would not let her leave. After her husband had been killed and the bank had taken over her ranch, she had moved to town and started her business. It had always been some satisfaction to her that Mrs. Tebo had made it possible for her to stay in Bald Rock.

Nan went along the hall to the sewing room in the back of the house. It was small, its double window facing the back yard with its big vegetable garden, the long lush rows without a single weed. Nan liked the room. It was sunny, filled with the smell of dress goods and usually cluttered with bright remnants. Nan dropped into a rocking chair, glancing at the sewing machine and dressmaker's dummy.

"You're busy?"

"Nothing pressing." Mary laughed. "The slave driver's giving a big party and wants this silk turned into a dress that will make her beautiful, but the party isn't till next week." She took the package from Nan and carried it to the cutting table. "Anyhow, I'd never be too busy to work on something for you."

"Except that I wouldn't let you. I don't need a dress. I just wanted one."

"Doesn't every woman?" Mary snapped the string and swept the paper aside. "Why, it's lovely, Nan. You'll look good in this." She eyed Nan a moment, then asked bluntly, "Is it for Rick?"

"I guess so."

"Get a pattern?"

"No."

Mary rummaged in a drawer in the sewing machine and found several that she gave to Nan. "Take your

65

choice."

Nan looked at them, rocking gently, and then glanced up. "Mary, I wanted to talk more than anything else. I've got myself into a corner."

"A woman never got into a corner she couldn't get out," Mary said. "I mean, if she's smart."

"I'm not that smart."

"I am." Mary's lips tightened. "I'm awful smart. You know, Nan, I used to think that it wouldn't take anything more than Spargo's funeral to make me happy. Seemed like there wasn't anything wrong with Chinook County that a good funeral wouldn't cure, but it's going to take more than Spargo's funeral to cure our troubles."

"There'll be some more."

"I've got a kettle of water on the stove. I'll make some tea."

Mary bustled into the kitchen. Nan went on rocking, idly studying the dress patterns. Presently Mary returned with cups, sugar, a pot of tea, and a plate of cookies.

"So you think there'll be more funerals." Mary poured the tea and set the cookies on the sewing machine within Mary's reach. "Who do you nominate for the guests of honor?"

"Joe Kinnear will do for one."

Mary nodded. "And Prine Tebo for another. I'd starve if it wasn't for what his wife gets out of him, but it would be worth it." She reached for a cooky. "Why pick on Joe except that he was thicker than fleas with Spargo?"

Nan told her what had happened the night before. Then she said, "I feel like I was caught in a fast river and can't swim, Mary. You can't reason with Grandpa. He says he wants to leave me a big spread, but I don't think it's really that. I—I think he's gone kind of crazy."

Mary's rocking chair squeaked under her. "Drink your tea," she said, "and keep talking. You haven't got around yet to what's on your mind."

"No." Nan stared at her cup. "How does it feel to be in love, Mary?"

"Now that's a crazy question. . . ." Mary checked herself. "Well, I don't know. Kind of quivery inside. Wanting a man so bad you wake up at night dreaming about him. I was that way about Hank before I married him. Seemed like I couldn't wait until we stood up before the preacher and got the knot tied."

"I know," Nan murmured. "I felt that way. After Rick kissed me the first time." She drank her tea and put the cup on the sewing machine beside the cookies. "But after you're married. What's it like then?"

Mary clicked her tongue and winked. "It's all you think it's going to be. If you get the right man, that is. It was with me, but I guess it's different with some women. Take our sanctimonious Mrs. Tebo. I get the notion when I talk to her that she sleeps with a rail between her and Prine, a good big one."

Nan rose and walked to the window. "There would be no rail between me and Rick."

"No, of course not." Mary took a long breath. "And then you might lose him. I never thought of that when I married Hank. I had three years with him. Awfully good years, Nan. Then they brought him in with his head busted. I don't know yet whether he was really throwed from that horse. He could ride anything with hair and hide on it. Sometimes I think he was murdered, but Cord Graham would never admit it."

"I wouldn't think about losing him," Nan said, her back to Mary. "I'd be thankful for three good years."

"You think that now, but they wouldn't be enough.

67

You get used to sleeping beside a man, feeling him right there with you and having him make you warm at nights when it's cold. You get so you plan for him. Cook for him and patch his clothes and . . . and everything. I'll never get used to being without Hank, Nan. I still wake up at night and put out a hand to see if he's there."

Nan turned. "I don't know what to do, Mary. It was different with you. Your folks had died and you had the ranch. I'm not saying that I want Grandpa to die, but I know it won't work out the way things are now."

Mary rocked furiously. "Nan Rawlins, if you love Rick like you're letting on, you won't hold back on account of Lou. I'll choke the old goat myself if it'd help."

"Don't talk like that."

"Why not?" Mary got up and walking to Nan, put an arm around her. "The world's made for young people. Don't you ever forget that. Lou's had his day to howl. He just won't realize that he's an old man and he's finished. If you love Rick and let him go, you'll hate yourself as long as you live."

"I don't know. I've told Rick a dozen times that if Grandpa won't stand for us getting married, I'll go away with him, but I don't think I can when the time really comes."

Mary dropped her arm. "Why not?"

"There's just me and Grandpa," Nan said tonelessly. "If I left him to go with Rick, and something happened to him, I'm afraid it would always be between us. I don't think I could forgive myself for that."

Mary chewed on her lower lip, head cocked. "It might be that way." She walked back to the cutting table and spread the organdie out, then she turned. "I'm not as smart as I was letting on. I'm just plain stupid in some

68

ways, but I do believe one thing. If you have a chance to be happy, and throw it away, you'll never forgive yourself for that."

"I suppose not." Nan walked to the sewing machine and picking up a pattern, handed it to Mary. "This will do."

Mary studied it a moment. "It'll look nice on you."

"There's Grant, too," Nan said. "I'm just not sure. He's good. He'd do anything for me."

"It's not enough unless you love him," Mary said with asperity. "Not near enough."

"He's older than I am," Nan went on as if not hearing. "When I was a little girl he used to come over and I'd sit on his lap. He let me ride his horse and he made whistles for me. He even took me hunting for rabbits. It would please Grandpa if I married him. He's talking about putting the outfits together."

"Oh, for goodness' sakes," Mary cried. "Are you getting married, or is it Lou?"

"Don't be foolish."

"I'm not. You either love a man or you don't. The trouble with you is you've minded Lou so long you can't break the habit."

"I guess that's right."

"Here, let's get this cut out. You'll feel better when you're inside a new dress. Hand me those pins."

Nan brought the pin holder from the sewing machine and laid it on the edge of the cutting table. She said, "I guess I don't know what I want. Maybe if Grandpa didn't shove Grant at me so hard, I'd like him. Like him enough to marry maybe."

"You feather-brained little fool," Mary breathed. "You let Rick make love to you and you told him you loved him, and now you say you don't know. You think

69

maybe it's Grant."

Nan dropped into the rocking chair, hands gripping its arms fiercely. "You think I'm not honest," she cried, "but it isn't that I'm just feathered-brained. I . . . I liked for Rick to kiss me and I thought I was in love with him, I'm all mixed up, Mary. I tell you I don't know."

"But all the time you knew Lou would raise Cain when he found out about you and Rick. All right, Nan. Look at yourself and tell me whether you're honest. Maybe Rick just gave you an excuse to rebel against Lou?"

"I guess so," Nan said miserably. "I got Rick to break up with Wildew and they'd been together for a long time. Tonight he's going to have it out with Grandpa and I know I can't go with him."

Mary sniffed. "You didn't do Rick any hurt when you got him to break up with Wildew." She pinned a piece of pattern on the organdie and picked up the scissors. Then she laid them back and turned to Nan. "What happened that made you see the light all of a sudden?"

"I don't know. Not exactly. It just hit me when we stopped at the Diamond J on our way into town. Grandpa's bound to drag Grant down with him, and it's wrong. Grant would be all right if Grandpa would let him alone. I got to thinking about it on the way into town. It was the first time I ever thought that . . . that maybe it's Grant I'm in love with."

"You're about as dependable as April weather," Mary said scornfully. "You just need to grow up."

"You don't know how I feel," Nan cried. "Marriage is so awfully permanent."

"It ought to be," Mary said softly. "It ought to be."

"I guess you didn't have any trouble making up your mind."

"That I didn't. It was Hank all the time. There never was any other man." Picking up the scissors, Mary whirled to the table and there was no sound for a moment but the steady whisper of the blades opening and closing on the cloth until she finished cutting the piece. Then she turned to Nan. "I don't know Rick very well, but I do know he's not like Wildew. Or Fleming and Cardigan. You're going to hurt him, Nan. That isn't right."

"I know," Nan breathed. "I know."

# CHAPTER 7

## "No" is the Answer

IT WAS AFTER ONE WHEN RICK AND THE OTHERS finished eating. Rawlins scooted back his chair. He said, "We'll try Tebo again. Grant, you'd better hike over to Mary's place and get Nan. I don't want her riding back home alone."

"She aimed to spend the day there," Rick said.

"She'll come," Rawlins said. "Get her horse out of the stable, Grant. We won't take long in the bank."

Nodding, Jenner rose. "I'll get the horse, but I ain't sure Nan will go."

"Then stay and ride back with her," Rawlins ordered.

Jenner walked out. Rawlins rolled a cigarette and fired it, his face grave. Wildew glanced at Rick, the cool, enigmatic smile on his lips, then looked at Rawlins. He said, his voice quite soft, "Let's get at it, Lou."

"Might as well." Rawlins grinned wryly. "I'm like a fellow with the toothache. Hurts like hell, but I don't

71

hanker to see the dentist, neither."

He rose and left the dining room, Rick and Wildew a pace behind him. They crossed the lobby and stepped out onto the boardwalk. The sun was not as bright as it had been that morning. Within the last hour clouds had rolled up over the Cascades to the west and had spilled out across the sky. The air was cool and heavy with rain smell, and thunder made a distant, ominous rumble.

"We'll get a wetting afore we get home," Rawlins said, and turned toward the bank.

"Malone."

Rick wheeled. It was Cardigan's voice, not at all soft now, and he had thrown the one word out like the crack of a blacksnake. Wildew said, "Git back, Lou."

"What the hell is going on. . . ." Rawlins began.

"Git back, Lou," Wildew repeated.

Rick lifted his Colt and checked it, and dropped it into leather again so that it rode easily in the holster. He was cool. It was one of the things he had learned from Wildew. "A lot of gunfighting is in your head," he always said. "Don't waste no time thinking about it. If you've got to worry, do it afterwards. When you pull a gun on a man, you'd better kill him, or you'll be hearing the devil talking to you."

"You want me, Deke?" Rick called.

Cardigan stood in front of the Stag, his thin body slack, face expressionless. He still had that deceptive softness about him, almost a feminine quality. It was one of his assets, for most men who faced him were inclined to underrate his ability. This was not true with Rick. He had seen Cardigan draw.

"I want you all right," Cardigan said. "You didn't figure on leaving town alive, did you, Malone?"

There was no point in talking now. It was another one

72

of Cardigan's assets, this talent for talking and playing for time while his enemy's nerves tightened. He was an old hand at the game, and in one regard he was like Wildew; either he was without fear or he appeared to be. Whichever way it was, the effect he had on the man he had planned to kill was the same.

"All right, Deke," Rick said, and moved around the hitch pole and into the street.

Cardigan had no choice then but to come off the walk. In this minute after Cardigan had first called, the street had been deserted. Rick faced the man, the distance between them growing less with each easy stride that Rick made. Cardigan stood motionless, waiting, right hand splayed above the butt of his gun.

There was no thought in Rick's mind now beyond this immediate job that must be done. Nan. Lou Rawlins. Matt Wildew. All of them were blotted out of his consciousness. His gun hung right. Not too low to waste a split second on the draw. Not too high so that the muzzle might catch when the gun was swept upward. His elbow slightly bent.

One step, the street shadowed momentarily as the sun was covered by a black cloud. Street dust was stirred by Rick's boots. Another step. Still Cardigan stood motionless, puzzled by the inexorable approach of the man he planned to kill. A third step, and someone coughed behind the batwings of the Stag, a loud sound in the pressing quiet.

Then Cardigan broke, hand whipping to gun butt and clutching it and lifting the Colt from leather. Rick had been warned, a warning that others who did not live by the gun would have missed. Wildew called it the "fire glow in their eyes." Rick caught it in Cardigan's eyes and he made his draw, thumb on the hammer, forefinger

73

on the trigger, grip on the butt tightening as the barrel cleared leather.

The shots were close together, Cardigan's just a little before Rick's, but still so close that the sound of them rolled out along the street as if they were one prolonged report. Rick felt the tug of a bullet as it slapped through his coat under his left arm. Cardigan went back under the hammering impact of the heavy slug.

Smoke hung above the street, then slowly faded as a breath of wind caught it, and the last echo of the shots died. The sun broke clear and in the sudden sharpening of the light Cardigan fell, his hands flung out, and dust lifted from the street as his slack body sprawled headlong into it.

Rick stood there, looking down at Cardigan and the gun that lay beside him, and the coolness was gone from him. Sweat broke through the skin of his face: he licked dry lips and suddenly he felt empty inside, terribly empty. It was always this way when he killed a man, and the thought of him, *I had nothing against Cardigan. It should have been Kinnear. Or Fleming.*

Men burst out of the buildings along the street and gathered around Cardigan's body, the doctor among them. It was always this way, too. They had been the audience to a grim drama, and now they were talking excitedly about what they had seen.

Rick wheeled toward Wildew and Rawlins who were standing at the corner of the hotel, Wildew's face impassive as if he'd had no interest in what had happened. Then Rick thought of something else Wildew had taught him and he swung back to the crowd. Cord Graham was there, saying, "All right, boys, get him off the street."

"What about it, Sheriff," Rick called, his gun still in

his hand.

Graham stared at him, his leathery face touched by regret. He would have liked it better, Rick thought, if it had gone the other way.

"Hell, you haven't got anything against him," Curly Hale shouted. "He couldn't have done nothing else."

Rick had not expected this from the Hatchet ramrod. Neither, apparently, had Graham. He snapped, "Shut your mouth, Curly." He nodded at Rick. "I ain't holding you."

Rick turned again and holstering his gun, walked to where Rawlins and Wildew stood. He said, "Sorry to hold you up, Lou."

Rawlins was leaning against the hotel wall in the manner of a man whose knees were too weak to hold him. He said, "You're mighty damned cool."

"Not so cool," Rick said. "I'll dream about it tonight maybe."

"You're good," Rawlins said. "I didn't know how good."

"I taught him," Wildew said. "We're both good. I told you that when we was hired."

"Yeah, I remember."

Rawlins straightened and went on toward the bank. Rick followed, glancing at Wildew, and again the thought prodded his mind that Wildew just didn't give a damn. If it had been another man, one who recognized the ties of friendship, he would have slapped Rick on the back; he'd have said he'd been worried and he was glad Rick had been both lucky and fast. But not Matt Wildew.

They went into the bank. Prine Tebo, standing at the window, turned to them, admiration in his eyes. He said, "That was a good job, Malone. I know what happened a

75

while ago between you and Fleming. I'm thanking you in case Lola never gets a chance to say it."

"I didn't expect that from you," Rick said.

"There are a few things you don't know." Tebo pinned his eyes on Wildew. "A man like Malone could stay here and make a place for himself. You never will."

"I'll make my place," Wildew murmured. "I ain't worried none."

"I came back to ask about that loan," Rawlins cut in. "I want to ask it a little different. Put it as a straight business proposition, Prine. You've got a lot of money invested in Hatchet. Now you've got a woman on your hands trying to run the outfit. Where does that leave your investment?"

"Right where it was," Tebo snapped. "Don't think you can put on Vance's boots, Lou. Ten years ago you wore 'em, but you can't fill 'em now."

"If anybody knows the cattle business, it's me," Rawlins shouted. "You hinting around that I don't?"

"No sense going over the ground again," Tebo said. "I've got my bank to think of, and I ain't betting a nickel of it on you. And if you try to take an inch of Hatchet range, Graham will throw you into the jug. I'll see to it."

"You aiming to play along with Lola?" Rawlins demanded.

"My business," Tebo said curtly. "You owe the bank money now. All your credit will stand and then some."

Rawlins reared back, his beard thrust defiantly at Tebo. "I ain't alone. You seen what Rick just done and you know what Wildew is. You can't brush me off like I was a sheep tick."

"I am brushing you, Lou," Tebo said wearily. "Get out."

76

"Wait," Rick said. "Suppose Lou here is willing to give you a mortgage on everything he owns. Suppose he asks you for about five thousand?"

Tebo was puzzled by the question and showed it. "I don't savvy. It'd take a hell of a lot more than five thousand for Lou to get the Hatchet herd."

"Suppose Grant Jenner wanted the same amount?" Rick asked. "Maybe give you the same deal."

"You're doing a hell of a lot of supposing," Tebo grumbled. "I just don't savvy what you're driving at."

"Last night Kinnear came out to the Bent R. He said for five thousand he'd see that Lou wouldn't get into trouble over Spargo's killing. He had made the same proposition to Jenner."

Tebo raised a blue-veined hand and brushed at his mustache, eyes moving to Rawlins and back to Rick. He said, "I hadn't heard about that, but it doesn't make any difference."

His voice held a grim note of finality. Wildew said, "We're wasting our wind, Lou."

Rawlins nodded and swung out of the bank. Tebo said, "Wait, Malone." Wildew lingered in the doorway, and went on when Tebo said, "I wanted Malone. Not you."

Rick asked, "Well?"

"I'm wondering about something," Tebo said. "I learned a long time ago that a banker had to judge a man's character as well as the collateral he had to offer when he asked for a loan. Lou's finished. You ought to be able to see that as well as I can. Just brooded over his bad luck so long he's loco. Now I don't give a damn about him, but I hate to see Jenner busted and there's Nan to think about, too."

It surprised Rick, and he wondered if he had been

wrong in mentally classing the banker with Kinnear and Cord Graham. He said, "Nothing will make Lou quit trying till he's dead."

"I know that. I just wanted to give you a piece of advice, Malone. Get out of it."

"I can't."

Tebo ran a hand through his hair, stirring it and leaving it rumpled. He said irritably, "I hate to see a man fighting on the wrong side, Malone. I mean the side that's wrong legally and morally. If you or Nan or maybe Jenner could get Lou to behave, there wouldn't be any trouble now that Spargo's dead."

"I take orders," Rick said. "I don't give 'em."

"Damn it, it's time you were giving some, then. I'm trying to say something, Malone. I'll put it this way. You came here with Wildew. Somewhere or other Jenner picked Fleming and Cardigan. Buzzards! That's what they are. Living off other men's troubles."

"I reckon that includes me."

"No," Tebo said. "That's what I'm saying. I figured you were like the others till I saw you handle Fleming. That makes it different. Maybe some of Wildew's cussedness has rubbed off on you, but it ain't hurt you none." He paused, lips tightening, and then added, "Yet."

Rick stared at the banker's somber face, the conviction growing in him that he had misjudged the man. He said, "I can't quit my job now. Anyhow, you're blaming the wrong man for the trouble we're going to have. Kinnear's the huckleberry who's kicking up the dust. He's started already."

Tebo turned away. "I'm sorry you think you've got to play your hand out with Lou."

Rick walked out of the bank, considering this, and

78

finding that his ideas about Bald Rock politics were upset. Rawlins and Wildew were waiting at their horses.

"What'd he want with you?" Rawlins demanded.

"He was hoping I could throw a rope on you," Rick said.

Rawlins laughed harshly. "Nobody can do that. Get your horse. We're riding."

"He's in the stable," Rick said, and moved past Rawlins.

"Malone."

It was the hotel clerk running across the street and waving an envelope at him. Rick stopped, asking, "What's biting you?"

"Miss Spargo." The clerk handed the envelope to him, smirking as if he could guess what was in it. "She said not to let you get out of town without giving you this."

"Thanks," Rick said, wondering.

The envelope was sealed. There was nothing written on it except his name in an even, legible hand. He waited until the clerk walked away, then tore the envelope open and took out the single sheet of paper that was in it. There was one sentence in the same handwriting as his name on the envelope: "I want to talk to you in my hotel room on a matter of mutual interest."

Rick put the note in his pocket. This was as crazy as Tebo wanting to talk to him alone in the bank. It might turn out to be the same thing. Lola Spargo probably thought he could put hobbles on Lou Rawlins.

Wildew and Rawlins had mounted, and Rawlins shouted in his irritable voice, "You getting that horse of your'n, Rick?"

"Later," Rick said. "Don't wait for me."

He crossed the street to the hotel, leaving them staring after him.

# CHAPTER 8

## Proposition

RICK PAUSED IN THE HOTEL LOBBY LONG ENOUGH TO turn the register and find the number of Lola's room. The clerk walked up, asking, "Anything I can do for you?"

Rick looked at the man, recognizing the lecherous sense of expectancy that was in him and remembering there had been some ugly gossip about Lola. He said, "No," and went up the stairs.

Lola opened the door at once to his knock. She said, "Come in," and stepped aside.

"I got your note. . . ."

"Come in," she repeated.

He walked into the room, not liking this and yet feeling that he should find out what she had in mind. She closed the door and motioned toward a chair. She said, "Sit down, Mr. Malone."

For a moment he stood there, looking at her. She was wearing a black dress and signs of grief were on her face, but still she retained a dignity of bearing and a beauty that would bring any man's eyes to her.

Without conscious thought, Rick found himself comparing her to Nan. They were totally unlike, but there was a difference that overshadowed all others. Nan was still a girl; Lola Spargo was fully matured, completely a woman. It struck Rick that a man would be lucky who had her love, and he wondered why she had never married.

"Please, Mr. Malone," Lola said. "Won't you sit

80

down?"

He turned to the chair and sat down as Lola crossed to the bed. For a moment she studied him, her dark eyes thoughtful as if she were mentally measuring him. He shifted uneasily, hand reaching for the makings and then dropping away.

"I know what you're thinking, ma'am," he said. "You're right. Men like me and Matt Wildew can be bought if you want to foot the bill."

"I'm sorry." She colored. "I didn't aim to look at you that way, but, well, the thing I'm going to say is unusual." She sat down on the edge of the bed. "Please smoke, Mr. Malone. I often wished I could. Men seem to think so much better with cigarettes in their mouths."

He rolled a smoke, grinning a little. "I guess that's right."

"First I want to thank you. I heard what that man said about me and I saw what you did. That's why I sent for you. You're not like Wildew. You're not like any other man I ever met."

He fished a match out of his vest pocket, frowning. "I don't savvy that. I'm just a gunslinger."

"No, you're not," she said warmly. "You did what you did because you had to and not because you thought you'd get paid for it."

"Why, sure . . ."

She raised a hand, smiling. "It set you apart. Don't you see? You're . . . well, I guess the word is chivalrous."

He fired his cigarette, frowning. "Nobody ever called me that before."

"I wanted to say it. Now that I've got it out of the way, I'll get down to business. I'm in trouble and I need help." She rose and walked to the window. "I don't

81

suppose you really knew Vance?"

"No."

"You know Joe Kinnear pretty well?"

"Well enough."

"Perhaps I'm prejudiced, but I think he's to blame for what Vance did and everything that's wrong with the valley. I hate to admit it, but I suppose that Vance got worse in the year I was gone. I blame Kinnear for that, too."

Rick doubted it. A man was what he was, and he had to bear the responsibility for his failings, but Rick didn't say it. It was natural for Lola to feel this way.

"I won't bother you about my past history or Vance's," Lola went on, "although I suppose you're prejudiced against us. Rawlins would give you only his side of it."

"I reckon," Rick agreed, not yet certain what she was getting at.

"I won't try to whitewash Vance," Lola said. "He was wrong. Terribly wrong, and he hurt a lot of people. I don't know whether he was guilty of murder, but he may have been. I do know the evil he did brought about his own murder. Perhaps there is a sort of justice to it. But then he was no worse than Lou Rawlins had been at one time and will be again if he has a chance."

"I won't argue on that."

She came back to the bed and sat down, smoothing her dress across her knees. "I can't prove it, but I have a feeling that Kinnear hired Fleming to say what he did. Of course he had no idea you'd jump into it."

"What makes you think Kinnear had anything to do with it?"

She was silent for a moment, her eyes on the floor. Then she forced herself to look at him. She said,

82

"People love to gossip. You've probably heard some about me."

"Nothing definite."

"But you've heard it. You see, Kinnear wants me to marry him and he has the idea that I can be forced into it. That's his way, Mr. Malone. Gossip is one thing that none of us can fight, especially a woman."

"From what I hear, Prine Tebo holds the top cards. You figure he dances to Kinnear's tune?"

"I'm not sure. I thought so, but he was very kind this morning. Maybe I've been wrong about him. I'm going to see him this afternoon before I leave town. That's what I wanted to talk to you about. I've got to fight. I just won't give up like Rawlins thinks I will and Kinnear hopes."

"Your brother stole most of what he had," Rick said bluntly. "With Tebo's help. You aim to keep it?"

"I aim to keep Hatchet," she said, "but not quite the way you imply. I'd undo the wrongs Vance did if I could, but it's foolish to think I can go back and set everything right. I will give Mary Dolan's place to her, but I can't bring her husband to life. Maybe he was murdered. If he was, I'm afraid Vance did it." She spread her hands. "When he was alive, he wouldn't listen to me. Now it's too late."

She was honest. He could not doubt that, and his respect for her grew. He nodded, "No, you can't go back and live his life over for him."

"What I'm getting around to saying is that letting Lou Rawlins grab Hatchet wouldn't help this country. Letting Kinnear go on running everybody's life is just as bad. You see, I've got something to fight for and not much chance of winning. I'll fight alone if I have to, but I need help. I'd like for you to work for me."

So that was it. He rubbed out his cigarette, considering this and realizing at once that it would set him against Rawlins and it would build a wall between him and Nan if nothing else did. But there was the other side of it, too. What Lola had said about Rawlins was right.

The time was coming when he had to make a choice. He would stay on the Bent R and find himself fighting for something he did not believe in, or he would quit. A decision like this would not worry Wildew; a few months ago it would not have bothered Rick, but now it did, and he was not sure why except that knowing Nan had given him some different ideas about a great many things.

"I can't," he said finally.

She leaned forward. "I said you weren't like Wildew. I mean that, I don't think you could fight for something you thought was wrong. Isn't that right?"

"I don't know," he said with sudden bitterness. "I mean, men like us don't do much thinking on them lines. It's like Rawlins told Wildew last night. He said he was paying him to fight, not to think." He spread his hands. "We just take orders."

"That's what's wrong with the world," she cried. "It's what's wrong with the valley. People just take orders, and keep right on letting Kinnear manage everything for his profit."

"I reckon your brother did."

"And I still say it's wrong. I don't claim to be unselfish about this. I need help and I'll pay for it. If it's a matter of money . . ."

He rose. "It ain't that. I just can't quit Lou now. Maybe he'll fire me." He grinned sourly. "If he does, well, it'd be a little different."

She got up and stood looking at him, her eyes almost level with his, and again he was impressed with the inherent honesty he sensed in her. She was far from the woman he had expected her to be, for he had supposed she would be much like Vance Spargo had been.

"Rawlins would never fire you," she said. "I guess I'm just reaching for straws. You get that way, you know, when you can't see any way out of your troubles."

"I wish I could help you. Maybe later . . ."

"It'll have to be now. I know Joe too well to think he'll wait." She hesitated, and then added, "There is one more thing. I can't get rid of a notion that Joe shot Vance. It's just a hunch, and I need help to prove it. I heard about the licking you gave him. He won't forget that."

"You're getting around to saying that we're on the same side whether we want to be or not. That it?"

She nodded. "There will be no in-between for any of us. Even Rawlins must know that."

"And Prine Tebo?"

"I'm not so sure. Maybe he's tied up with Kinnear so he can't get loose."

"What about your crew?"

"I don't know. Most of the men are new. I'll find out about that, too."

"Curly Hale?"

"He's the one man I can count on. He's ridden for Hatchet for years and I know he thought a lot of Vance. He likes me, too, but he can't do much alone. It's money. I mean, it boils down to that, and I don't have much time to raise it. Curly's the kind of man who needs someone he respects like Vance who will give him orders." She smiled, her head held high and proud.

"I was hoping you'd be the one."

She wouldn't beg. He liked that about her, and it seemed to him that here was the chance he had been looking for. He had broken with Wildew because of Nan, but the break would have come in time anyhow. Six years had not made him into another Matt Wildew, six years that had been wasted while discontent had grown in him. The events of the last few hours had brought all the things that had been wrong with his past into sharp focus.

He wheeled to the door, knowing that he had to get out of here. Then, with a hand on the knob, he looked back. Her face was composed, masked against the disappointment that he knew was in her.

"I hope you win," he said.

"As it stands now," she said, "I don't have a chance. Fighting isn't a woman's job."

He went out, closing the door behind him. The last glimpse he had of her would stay with him, her head held in that high, proud way. As he went down the stairs, he felt the keen edge of regret. She possessed a rare kind of courage, and that stood high in Rick's standard of values.

It would be very simple for her to surrender and marry Kinnear; she would have all the things handed to her that most people fought to acquire. Still, she was turning them down. He wondered what choice Nan would make if she faced such a decision.

The clerk was loitering in front of the desk when Rick reached the lobby. He glanced at Rick, grinning. "Quite a woman, ain't she, Malone? Quite a woman."

There was no mistaking his meaning. Rick hit him, knocking him sprawling against the desk. He pulled himself upright and put his back to the desk, his face filled with outrage.

"What'n hell did you do that for?" he shouted. "Everybody knows what she is. Don't tell me you ain't after what any man wants out of a woman."

Rick took a step toward him, wanting to yank him to his feet and hit him again. He stopped. He could not change the fellow's opinion of Lola, and he could not stop his tongue from wagging. He swung on his heel and left the lobby.

Within ten minutes Rick was on his way out of town, forgetting about Nan and Jenner until he was opposite the Hatchet buildings. He didn't turn back. Jenner would stay and come with Nan, and Rawlins and Wildew had probably gone on ahead.

Now, thinking about what Lola had told him, he realized more fully than he had before that he would reach his own decision tonight. He wondered if his love for Nan was enough to tie him to Lou Rawlins an his crazy, futile scheme, and realized it wasn't.

Nan would not understand that, but it was something he had wanted to do for a long time. Now it was the thing he must do. He could only hope that when the moment came for Nan to make her choice, she would be able to see it his way.

# CHAPTER 9

## Unexpected Ally

LOLA HAD NOT REALLY EXPECTED RICK MALONE TO say anything different from what he had. Some men could shift their loyalty without effort, but Malone was not such a man, and she respected him for it. If Rawlins

87

did fire him and he came to her, she was certain he would go through to the finish. She moved to the window, smiling derisively at this wild hope. Rawlins would not fire a man like Rick Malone.

She remained there at the window until she saw Rick leave town, riding easily as a man does who has spent much of his waking hours in the saddle. Her eyes followed him until he was lost to sight. Just watching him sent a strange, warm glow through her. As long as she lived, she would never forget the terrifying prickle that ran down her spine when she had heard what Fleming said. She had wanted to run, to get away from the eyes of the men who had heard Fleming, men who probably regarded her the same way he did.

Then she had heard the commotion behind her. Impulsively she had looked back to see Malone handle Fleming in the hard, brutal way of a man who is no stranger to violence. She had fled into the hotel, panic crowding her.

Later she had watched the gunfight between Malone and a man she did not know, and she had guessed that it had come out of the trouble with Fleming. Rick had survived. She would always thank God for that. She would never have forgiven herself if he had died because of the impulsive gesture he had made for her.

Now, staring into the street, it came to her that she would be safe from the kind of talk Fleming had made, at least within her hearing. She owed that to Rick Malone and she would be eternally grateful. Perhaps in some way she could repay him. There were too few men in the world like him. If he went on working for Rawlins, he'd end up in jail, or dead. Whichever way her fight with Kinnear went, Lou Rawlins was bound to lose. Prine Tebo had assured her of that.

She glanced at her watch. It was after three. Curly Hale was coming for her with a livery rig at four. He had sent the crew back to the cow camp and she had told him she had some things to do and would not be ready to leave town until later in the afternoon.

She left her room, feeling depressed because she had failed with Malone. She knew now she had pinned more hope on him than she had realized. Prine Tebo was in his office and there were no customers in the bank. She was thankful for that. She did not feel like waiting. Tebo was her one remaining hope, a slim one, for she could not count on him any more than she had been able to count on Rick Malone.

Tebo called her into his private office and motioned to a chair. He stepped around her and sat down at his desk so that he could watch the bank. She dropped into the chair, folding her hands on her lap, eyes on Tebo's tight-lipped mouth, and the weight of failure was heavy. Kinnear was right. Tebo owed something to his bank, and he would not believe she could run Hatchet as Vance had done, even with Curly Hale's loyal help.

"You've had a hard day," Tebo said in a kindly voice. "You look tired."

"It was a long trip from The Dalles," she said, "and I couldn't sleep very well last night."

He nodded gravely. "Of course. There doesn't seem to be any justice in Vance dying now with most of his life before him." He hesitated, and then added, "But he'd changed. He wasn't the man he had been. I don't know what happened to him. He had enough to satisfy most men, but not Vance. Even threatened Rawlins and Jenner. If they hadn't brought in some gunfighters, I think he'd have raided their ranches."

Tebo knew what had been wrong with Vance, she

thought, but she didn't say it because it was the same thing that was wrong with him and with Cord Graham. Instead she said, "Gunfighters wouldn't have stopped Vance if he really wanted to run Rawlins and Jenner out of the country."

Tebo shrugged. "You never can be sure of what might have happened if he'd lived. We've got enough trouble without thinking of what might have been."

"You mean I have the trouble." She leaned forward. "I came in to find out how I stand. Joe told me last night that Hatchet was in debt and you'd close me out."

The banker flushed. He tapped the desk top with the tip of his fingers, a steady drumming sound that irritated Lola. Then he rose and began pacing around his office, hands deep in his pants' pockets.

"Damn it, Lola," Tebo said finally, "I'm in a pinch. I backed Vance because I believed he was the best cowman in the valley, and the little fellows between him and the Bent R had borrowed from the bank until they were in over their heads. A lot of folks think we did wrong, but I had to protect my bank. I knew that when times got better, Vance would pull himself out. The little fry never would. They just didn't have the savvy."

"About Hank Dolan," she murmured. "Some say he was murdered. That happened just before I left, you know."

"Gossip," Tebo said savagely. "Been a lot of it about me and Vance. About Kinnear, too. Law enforcement isn't my business, but I'm convinced that Hank's death was not accidental."

Tebo's face was haggard. It surprised Lola. She had never been on intimate terms with Tebo, and she had always regarded him as a cold-blooded banker with an eye on the easy dollar wherever he could find it. Now

90

she sensed the worry that was in him, and it struck her that the things he and Vance had done were weighing heavily upon him.

"What about Hatchet?" she asked.

He sat down in his swivel chair again and fumbled in his pocket for a cigar. He said, "Did you come back with any money?"

"About two hundred dollars," she said. "It was all I could save."

"Not enough. Vance left less than five hundred in his checking account." Tebo bit off the end of his cigar and chewed on it a moment. "Hatchet has no assets except land, which is mortgaged for all it's worth, and cattle. Right now the market for cattle is bad. Might be better by fall, but chances are it'll come too late to help you."

"How much do I owe?"

"I couldn't say offhand," he answered evasively, "but it's more than you can hope to raise. Vance was a plunger. It would have worked out all right if he'd lived. The bank inspector never questioned the loans I had made to Vance, but it's different now. I think you can see that."

"I'll pay you," she said in a low tone. "Some way. Maybe we could make an arrangement for you to take back the other places Vance had and I could keep the home ranch."

Tebo shook his head. "It's all tied up together." He paused, looking at her thoughtfully, then asked, "Lola, are you going to marry Joe?"

"I'll never marry him," she said evenly. "I think you know why."

"I can guess." Tebo rose, his cold cigar still in his mouth. "I don't want to hurt you, Lola, but I'm in a pinch and that's the truth."

He began to pace around the room again, his face gray and old, and she could not help believing him. She asked, "Would it help if I could raise the interest?"

"If you could raise it all." He stopped, his eyes on her. "It didn't help you none when Rawlins started getting big notions. He hasn't got much chance of pulling off a big grab, but with these gunmen around, he could be mighty nasty. With things the way they are, I can't depend on a woman keeping Rawlins off Hatchet range."

"I can understand that," she said. "Who was the man that was killed?"

"Deke Cardigan." He walked back to the desk, looking intently at her. "You know what caused that fight?"

"I think so." Her hands were closed tightly; she felt sweat break through the skin of her palms, making them damp and clammy. This was the last thing she wanted to talk about, but she knew she had to. "Has this gossip got anything to do with me keeping Hatchet?"

"Not a bit." He shook his head, smiling at her. "Lola, if I had a daughter, I'd want her to be like you."

She had not expected an answer like that, and she felt a sudden warmth rush through her. "Thank you, Mr. Tebo. It's been pretty hard, you know."

"Of course it has." He sat down again. "I know exactly what Joe Kinnear is. I'm going to talk honestly and depend on you not telling anyone what I've said. You would ruin me if you did."

"I'm not one to talk," she said. "I've been on the other end of it too long."

"My life hasn't been a happy one." He chewed fiercely on his cigar, a finger tip making a series of ovals on his desk top. "I'm not complaining or asking

92

for sympathy, but it's true. You know my wife. I wanted children and she didn't. Well, like a lot of men, I found another woman. Joe knows about her. Gossip would hurt both of us. I can't afford to let it get out." He looked up, suddenly defiant. "You won't understand this, but a man in my position is supposed to have a good reputation. Morally, I mean. You know what the old women of the valley would do if they got their tongues on me."

She nodded. "I should know."

"Well, that's what puts me in a corner," he said glumly. "Joe cracks the whip and I jump. He wants to run for Congress and he wants you to show off as his wife. He wants Hatchet, too. He looks a long ways ahead. Always has. Now he's reaching for the plums. He's been nursing the tree for a long time."

"I hate him," she breathed. "Why does he think he can force me to marry him?"

"Because he has always forced other people. It's the only thing he understands. Take me. Or Cord Graham. He uses any weapon he can find. He's got money. Last year he bought into the bank so he'd know what went on."

She felt that Tebo wanted to help her. More than that, she was sure he hated Kinnear as much as she did. Because she was certain, she said, "We both want to be free of him. Isn't that right?"

He nodded. "I've been down on my knees to him so long I've got calluses on them. I think that someday I'll kill him." He slammed the cigar down on the desk, brooding eyes pinned on her. "Well, I've talked too much. If you were to let this out . . ."

"I won't, Mr. Tebo. I'm worrying about myself and Hatchet. There must be some way for us to work together."

He was an old and beaten man, and he made no effort to mask the misery that was in him. He said, "I've thought about it ever since Vance was killed. I have one small hope to offer, but it's so small I hesitated to mention it."

"What is it?" she asked eagerly.

"I was wondering about this man Malone. I saw him go into the hotel. Did you talk to him?"

She nodded. "After what happened, I thought he might help me, but he won't quit Rawlins."

"I'm sorry. At a time like this one man can make a great deal of difference."

"Just fighting won't help us, Mr. Tebo. What was your idea?"

He rose again, his hands shoved in his pants' pockets. "Hale will see you through this, but your crew can't be depended on as long as Kinnear is alive and capable of paying them to walk out on you." He began to walk, not looking at her. "They're building a railroad south from the Columbia. As far as Moro anyway. Construction men eat lots of beef. There's a long chance you could sell and deliver a small herd to them this fall before your interest is due."

"Kinnear will stop us."

"That's why you need a man like Malone." Tebo put out a hand in a pleading gesture. "Suggest this to Hale as if it was your idea. If Kinnear found out I'd ever done or said anything to help you, he'd ruin me."

Lola got up, understanding how much Tebo's fear of Kinnear had shaped his life. She said, "You're afraid of Joe, but Vance wasn't. Since I've been back, I've wondered if Vance rebelled against him and he shot him."

94

"I believe he did."

"Have you told Graham?"

"Of course not. I said I believe he did. It wouldn't do any good anyhow. Kinnear owns Graham."

She remembered the look on Kinnear's face the night before when she'd said he had killed Vance. The more she thought about it, the more she was convinced that that expression had been an admission of guilt. Now Tebo had frankly stated the same suspicion.

"Was there any trouble between them?"

"Not that I know of, but there was one thing which might have made trouble."

"What?"

"You."

She picked up her reticule, her lips trembling. She had not thought of it before, but now she was sick with the knowledge that she might have been responsible for Vance's death. She said dully, "I guess I should have married Joe."

"No." Tebo came to her and took her hands. "Listen, Lola. Vance loved you. Don't ever forget that. After you left, he finally got it through his head how you felt about Joe, and I think he began to see that Joe was not the man he thought he was. None of us did at first. You know Joe has a talent for talking about what's good for all of us when he's thinking about what's good for him."

"When I left Vance wanted me to marry Joe."

"I know, but he changed his mind. I know because he talked to me about it. Joe tried to make him ask you to come back. That was a mistake. Vance was one man Joe couldn't make do anything. When it came to you, Vance wouldn't budge."

"Joe knew that I'd come if Vance was killed."

"And he was confident he could make you knuckle

95

down. The harder it is for Joe to get something, the more he wants it."

She bowed her head, fighting back the tears that were very close. She had broken down when they had lowered the coffin into the grave. Now she was afraid she was going to again. Suddenly she whirled and started out of Tebo's office.

"Lola."

She turned back, her chin trembling. He looked at her, his eyes level with hers. He said gently, "We'll lick him, Lola. Someway."

"It's wrong," she whispered. "So terribly wrong. We both think he killed Vance, but still the law won't even look into it."

"Maybe not the law," Tebo said, "but he'll die. I'll kill him. Or you'll kill him. Or somebody will. He doesn't have a real friend in the valley. Oh, he can get folks to vote the way he wants them to, but that doesn't make them friends. He's like a wild animal in the timber who makes the others afraid of him. Sooner or later he'll be pulled down."

"But maybe not soon enough."

She turned and this time he let her go. It was almost four when she reached her hotel room. She packed the valise she had opened, leaving her coat out, for the storm would break in a few minutes. When she returned to the lobby, Curly Hale was waiting for her, a livery rig in the street.

Hale put her valises in the bed behind the seat, stepped up beside her and took the lines from the whipstock. He said, "We're going to get wet."

"It isn't far," she said.

They left town at a brisk pace, Hale glancing up at the sullen sky. Lightning ran across it in jagged bursts of fire and thunder boomed at them, then the first big drops hit them and Hale muttered, "Should have waited."

Lola glanced at him, thinking that here was the one man whose loyalty she would never question, the one man Vance had kept, even though Kinnear must have wanted him out of the way. Hale was about fifty, a tall gangling man with the bowed legs and weather-scarred face of one who had spent most of his life in the saddle.

"What chance have we got to save Hatchet?"

"None."

He said it with grim finality. She glanced at him again, it was raining hard now, drops running down his face and around the big mole on the end of his nose and some dripping off the end of his flowing yellow mustache. She felt the rain on her hair and face, and she shivered, feeling a sudden chill.

"What can we do, Curly?"

"Dunno. Been wondering ever since Vance died. Look's to me like Tebo's gonna take Hatchet, the damned money hound."

She looked ahead at the slanting silver lances of rain that had blotted out the rimrock on both sides of the valley. She said nothing more until Hale swung off the road and drove up the lane that led to the Hatchet buildings. He pulled up in front of the house, saying, "Get inside." She jumped down and ran across the porch and into the house.

Hale brought her valises, asking as he came through the front door, "Your old room?"

"Of course."

He carried the valises upstairs, boots leaving muddy tracks on the floor and stairs. When he returned, he said, "Get them duds off. I'll start a fire."

She was soaked. Now she shivered, although the

house had been closed all day and still held the heat of the warm morning. She started walking around the living room, touching the oak table Vance had freighted south from The Dalles years ago. She fingered through the pile of old papers and magazines and the mail-order catalog; she looked at the chairs and the black leather couch and the bear rug in front of the fireplace.

It was hard to believe she had been gone for more than a year. The room looked exactly as it had when she'd left, even to the guns hung across the antlers on the wall. She should be hearing Vance's great voice and hearty laugh. A chill ran down her back. This had been her home for years, long before Vance had known Joe Kinnear and let his overweening greed change him. She could not give it up. Whatever Vance had done, this was her home.

She heard pine kindling snapping in the kitchen range. Hale tramped back into the living room, boot heels cracking on the floor. He shouted, "Hod dang it, get them wet clothes off. You trying to catch cold?"

"Curly, I'm going to save Hatchet."

He shook his head and brought a hand across his face and wiped his mustache. "You can't. Vance fixed that. He had the fool idea the sky was the limit. Even if the price of beef was up, you'd have a hard time paying the bank off."

"I'm going to save it," she said doggedly. "Some way. I talked to Tebo this afternoon. If we could raise the interest, he'll give us more time."

"And how are you going to do that?"

"Tebo said . . ." She checked herself. "Before I left The Dalles, I heard about a railroad that's being built south of the Columbia. I want you to start out in the morning and go up there. See if you can make a dicker

98

with them. They'll be buying beef from somebody to feed their construction crews. Might as well be Hatchet beef."

He wiped his mustache again, looking at her uneasily as if he thought it was a fool's errand at best. Then he asked, "What was it Tebo said?"

"He said he'd give us more time if we can meet the interest. I guess that would satisfy the bank inspector."

"Inspector, hell," Hale snorted. "That ornery son wants Hatchet. I'll bet my bottom dollar he's the one who plugged Vance so he could close us out."

"Will you try?"

He took off his Stetson and scratched his bald head. "All right," he said grudgingly. "I'll start tonight. Ain't far. Maybe I can get back by tomorrow evening." He walked to the door. "'I've got to take that rig to town and I'll fetch some grub home. Not much left in the pantry."

"It's still raining."

"I've been wet before," he said testily. "Now are you gonna get them duds changed, or ain't you?"

"Right away," she said, and went up the stairs.

Her room was just as she had left it. Again she had the weird feeling that she had been gone but a few days. She stood at the window and watched Hale drive out of the yard and presently the silver curtain of rain blotted him from her sight.

She began to undress. The house was very still. She shivered again, unable to shake off the feeling that soon she would hear Vance yell at her the way he used to, "I'm coming in, Sis. You decent?"

She had not been chilled enough to be cold, but she continued to shiver. She opened a bureau drawer and took out a maroon robe that Vance had given her the

Christmas before she'd left. She knotted the cord around her and took down her hair, gaze swinging around the room. There was the old familiar crack in the wallpaper, the same lace spread over her bed, the leather-bottom rocking chair, even Kinnear's picture on the bureau beside Vance's.

With a sudden rush of temper, she picked Kinnear's picture up and threw it into the hall. She went out and kicked it down the stairs. Returning, she sat down in front of the bureau and looked at herself in the mirror. Her hair hung down her back in a dark, stringy mass. She picked up her brush and ran it through her hair, then she stopped. A sense of loneliness gripped her and she began to cry.

# CHAPTER 10

## Fired

RICK WAS ALMOST TO THE DOLAN PLACE JUST BELOW Jenner's Diamond J when he felt the first drop of rain. Thunder had been booming across the sky for half an hour and he knew he was going to be caught by the storm before he reached the Bent R. Then he heard the sharp crack of a rifle.

For an in instant he thought the shot was another burst of thunder. He had not expected trouble, and he had been riding carelessly, his thoughts on Nan. Then he identified the sound and wheeled his horse off the road, cracking steel to him.

He heard the second bullet, a hornet-like *zing* close to the side of his head. The valley was narrow here, and as he plunged through the willows along the river, he realized that the rifleman was on the rimrock to the south. He must have been waiting there, knowing Rick would ride by.

Pulling up in the shallow water at the edge of the stream, Rick yanked his Winchester from the boot and piled off. The willows would not give him any real protection, but they would screen him so he couldn't be seen from the rim and only a lucky bullet would tag him. He dropped belly flat on the gravel and wormed his way back into the willows until he could see through them. There he waited, eyes on the grim, flat line of the south rim.

There was no movement up there, no sound that reached Rick's ears except the hammering of big raindrops against the willow leaves around him. The first bullet had been wide, the second close, so close that there could be no doubt of the rifleman's murderous intentions. The fellow wasn't a good shot, but he's tried.

Rick's first thought was of Kinnear. He decided against the lawyer at once. He was by nature a careful and scheming man. He'd be in town where he could establish an alibi that would keep him above suspicion. Fleming? Probably, Rick thought. After Cardigan's failure, Fleming would have no stomach to face the man who had killed him, but he was not one to forget the horse-trough treatment he had received.

The rifleman opened up again, slugs coming in low and slapping through the willows. Rick scooted back toward the river and dug his face into the gravel. One bullet kicked up sand and small rocks to his left, the others were wide. The fellow was spreading his shots, guessing what Rick had done and, hoping for a lucky hit.

The firing stopped again. Rick crawled forward,

studying the rimrock. The rain was coming down hard now, blurring the air so that the rim was indistinct. Rick could not catch the faintest trace of powdersmoke. The man was probably lying behind a boulder, or between two of them. Rick could stay here till sundown and not catch a glimpse of the drygulcher.

Rick slipped back to the edge of the water and rose. Wildew was right in saying that it was stupid to make an enemy and leave him alive. Too late now, Rick thought as he slipped the Winchester into the boot and swung into saddle. He could leave the country, or expect to be shot by the bushwhacker. It was not a pleasant choice.

Keeping inside the willows, he followed the edge of the water until he reached a shallow riffle and put his horse across it to the north bank. By the time he reached the hay field that lay along the river, the rain was coming down so hard that both arms were blotted from sight. Now anger began to rise in him. He'd hunt Fleming down and kill him. He'd have to if he stayed here.

By the time he reached the Bent R he was soaked to the skin. The others had returned. The buggy was in the yard, Nan's and Wildew's horses in the corral, and Jenner's animal in front of the house. He put his horse away and slogged through the mud to the back door of the house, his temper drawn fine.

This was the first time in his life that he had been shot at from ambush. Wildew had always managed to call the turn, for he went on the proposition that a man should stay out of trouble until it was time for the showdown. When that moment came, you kept your enemies in front of you and you killed them, or you stayed under cover until you could.

Rick knocked mud from his boots and went in. They were all in the kitchen, the men sitting at the table, Nan standing beside the stove, and Rick felt the welcome warmth from the fire and smelled the coffee. They eyed him for a moment, no one saying anything, then Nan asked in a low tone, "Coffee?"

"Sure." Rick pinned his eyes on Wildew. "Have your laugh, Matt. Somebody just tried to plug me from the rimrock."

Nan cried, "Oh!"

No one seemed to hear her. "Where?" Rawlins asked.

"Just below the Dolan place."

"Looks like he was a bad shot," Wildew said, grinning. "Well, there were some things you couldn't learn. Who do you figure it was?"

"Fleming."

Wildew nodded agreement. "Chances are you're guessing right. He'll try again. You'd better go crawl under your bunk and stay there where you'll be safe."

"I'll have that cup of coffee first," Rick said.

Nan poured it and handed the cup to him, her eyes lowered. She said, "They told me what happened in town."

"Fool stunt," Rawlins said ominously. "Now you've got Fleming gunning for you, and we've got enough trouble without piling that on to the rest."

Wildew kept on grinning in his cool distant way as if he found this amusing. Jenner, his face more red than pink, was staring at the floor. Nan was flustered and worried. Rawlins was angry, so angry that he was about to blow up and tongue-whip Rick for jumping Fleming.

The uneasy silence went on for a full minute. Rick drank his coffee, sizing each of them. up, and reaching a decision that was long overdue. He said, "Lou, I can't go along on this, and I don't think Matt will. You can't pay us enough to get shot for a fool deal that you haven't got a chance to pull off."

It was blunt, too blunt, but Rick was in no mood to take the long way around. Rawlins got up and kicked his chair back, beard thrust at Rick in the belligerent way he had when someone opposed him.

"I'll talk for myself, kid," Wildew said.

"And I'll do some talking," Rawlins shouted. "When it gets down to cases, you leave me high and dry. You pull out with your tail between your legs like a damned, yellow-bellied . . ."

"Grandpa," Nan cried. "Stop it."

"You're talking wild, Lou," Jenner said with more heat than his voice usually held. "There's nothing yellow about Malone. He showed that today and what he just said makes sense."

Rawlins wheeled on him. "I ain't asking for your put in. I aimed to get them papers drawn up today, but I forgot it, getting worked up over Tebo like I done, but I'll tell you what I did last spring when Spargo told us what we could expect. I had Kinnear draw up a will. I'm leaving the Bent R to you and Nan, share and share alike, and I expect you two to get married."

"That's not right, Grandpa," Nan said in a low, bitter voice. "Have you got to beat me down like you do other people? I told you once today that I won't be haggled over like a . . . a heifer you'd sell to Grant. I meant it."

Rawlins stood with his back to her, staring at Jenner. He said, "I'm an old man, Grant. I want to leave the Bent R in good hands, and you've been more'n a neighbor to me. Don't walk out on me now."

Jenner rose, his face haggard. "You know how I feel about Nan, but I don't want her this way."

"She'll come around," Rawlins said brusquely. "We'll go back to town tomorrow and draw up them partnership papers. Sorry I forgot it today, but it don't make no real difference. I've been thinking on this. We don't have to have Tebo's backing, and we don't need money to buy more cattle. We'll take Hatchet range regardless. Lola can't do nothing. What's more, if I've got that Hatchet crew sized up right, they won't do no fighting."

"What are you figuring on now?" Jenner asked in a ragged voice.

"What I should have done today without running into town and begging for a loan from that damned Tebo. We'll go to the cow camp in the morning, you'n me and Wildew. That'll make nine of us with our boys. It's enough. We'll round up our steers. Nobody'll bother the cows and calves for a few days. We'll leave 'em right where they are and we'll drive the steers on to Hatchet range. I'm betting my bottom dollar that the first cap we crack will send every Hatchet man in the outfit running over the hill so fast we won't see nothing but dust."

It was fantastic. Rick stared at the old man's gaunt figure, convinced that Cord Graham had been right. Rawlins' bad luck had made him loco. He had lost all capacity to reason; he had made up his mind and he'd go on to the bitter end, unable to see that he could do nothing but bring injury and defeat and heartbreak to those who loved him.

"I dunno . . ." Jenner began.

"I do," Rawlins snapped. "I've decided on it. By fall you'll see I'm right. Tebo's got to have somebody on Hatchet who knows cattle. Once he sees we mean business, he'll come around."

"You're an old fool," Rick said. "Likewise you're a

stubborn mule-head who can't see past the end of your nose."

Rawlins swung to face him, his weathered face turning red with the sudden rage that burned through him. "Get out. I forgot you was still here. Pack your war bag and get to hell off the Bent R. You're fired."

"You're too late. I fired myself a while ago, but there's one thing you don't know." Rick stepped to Nan's side and put an arm around her. "Nan and me are going to get married. If you want her, you've got to take me. I'll work, Lou, if you quit this crazy scheming. I'm done hiring out my gun."

Rawlins' mouth sagged open. He looked at Nan, expecting a denial. He blurted, "It ain't true. You're all I've got, Nan, just you and Grant. Tell me it ain't true."

She stood beside Rick, her slim body tense under his arm, her face pale. "I've got a right to make up my own mind, Grandpa. Seems like you just can't understand that."

"You don't have to throw your life away on a gunslinger." Rawlins took a step toward her. "You've got no kin but me, Nan, and you're all the kin I've got. Everything I've done and all the plans I've made are for you."

"But it never has occurred to you that I have my own plans," she whispered. "You never think about me having any feelings. It's . . . it's always been that way as long as I can remember."

He came to her, ignoring Rick, and putting his hands out, took her. There were tears in his eyes. Rick, his arm still around Nan, sensed that this had shocked Rawlins as nothing else could have done. If Nan walked out, there would be no reason for him to keep on living. For the first time it came to Rick that the old man's fantastic desire to bring the Bent R back to its former glory was prompted by his love for Nan as much as his desire of wealth and power.

"Nan," Rawlins said in a low, begging voice. "Nan, honey, don't leave me. It's the only thing I can't stand."

She looked up at Rick, biting her lower lip. "I can't go with you, Rick. Don't you see?"

He pulled his arm away from her and stepped back. In that moment he felt no anger. Just hurt, the kind of hurt he could not describe. An ache, a dull, pressing ache that made it hard to breathe. He thought, *She doesn't know what she's doing. In the pinch there's nobody but him.*

"You promised," he said in a low tone. "You said that if he wouldn't put up with me, you'd go away."

"But can't you see, Rick?" she cried.

"I just see one thing. You're turning me down for him."

She lowered her gaze. "We can wait till this is all over. It'll be different then."

"It'll never be different as long as he's alive," he said bitterly. "You love me or you don't."

"I don't love you enough to break his heart," she said.

"You were just having a little fun with me. That it?"

"If you won't even try to understand how I feel," she flared, "I guess you don't love me very much."

He was not really surprised. From the time they had stopped at the Diamond J that morning the feeling had grown in him that it would go this way. Without a word he wheeled out of the kitchen and crossed the yard to the bunkhouse. He told himself he'd never love another woman. Wildew had been right about her. Maybe he had been right about some other things. Like buying a woman when he wanted one.

It did not take long to pack his war bag. He had been here a few months, as long as he had stayed anywhere since he had started traveling with Wildew. It had been a home of sorts, as much of a home as he had known since his mother had died when he was fourteen and he had started drifting. But it had turned out to be just another job. Now it was behind him.

Like an ordinary cowhand, Rick's "thirty years' gatherin's" could be packed into a flour sack. It didn't take long. A hair rope he had been pleating in the few odd moments he'd had here on the Bent R, some whang leather, a needle and thread, an extra pair of spurs, shaving gear, and a few other odds and ends. He rolled the flour sack up in his tarpaulin along with his soogans and the clothes he wasn't wearing, and carried it to the corral.

The storm was over, the clouds rolling on toward the Blue Mountains to the east, and most of the sky was clear with the sun well down to the west. There was a moist, washed smell in the air, and steam was rising from a soaked earth. By the time Rick had saddled and tied his bedroll on his extra horse, Wildew had come to stand beside the corral, a cigarette dangling from his mouth.

"So you've decided to change your bedding ground," Wildew said with lazy indolence.

"I didn't decide it," Rick said darkly. "It was decided for me. Rub it in, Matt. Go ahead. Rub it in."

Wildew laughed. "No, I ain't made that way. I thought you knew me better'n that."

Rick stood beside his saddle horse, looking at Wildew. It was at if these six years had never been. Matt Wildew was a stranger, a slender, pale-eyed stranger with the tough face of a killer. At that moment

Rick felt neither affection nor dislike for the man.

"I don't know you," Rick said. "I don't know you at all."

Wildew shrugged. "Right now you've been hit a purty hard lick and you're out of your head. Tomorrow it'll be different. Where you headed?"

Rick hadn't thought about that. He'd just wanted to get off the Bent R. Now he remembered the job Lola Spargo had offered him, a good job that gave him something to fight for that he could believe in. No matter what Wildew had tried to teach him, the gunman had never made him over in his own image. He'd take the job on Hatchet. He'd told Lola that if Rawlins fired him, it would be different. Well, he'd been fired.

"I'll be on Hatchet."

It was seldom that Wildew showed any surprise, but he did now. He looked sharply at Rick, puzzled, then he murmured, "Well, I'll be damned. You sure?"

"I'm sure."

"There's Fleming," Wildew said pointedly. "And Kinnear ain't gonna cotton to the idea of your hanging around his girl."

"Didn't figure he would. I reckon that's why I'm going to Hatchet. I've got a few things of my own to settle before I leave this range."

Wildew flipped his cigarette away. "I didn't figure you'd run, but fighting ought to pay a man."

"I'll get paid."

"Big?"

Rick shrugged. "Dunno. That ain't important."

"You saw the Spargo woman before you left town. That it?"

Rick nodded. "She thinks Kinnear killed her brother."

"Well now, that makes everything fine." Wildew

shook his head. "Don't go off half-cocked, kid. I still say there's a big deal here. I ain't sure yet just how to work it, but it's here, and I'll get my teeth into it before I'm done. Changed your mind about getting in?"

"No." Rick mounted. "Just one thing, Matt. I'll take care of Fleming and Kinnear when the sign's right. Lola figures Kinnear put Fleming up to saying what he did about her. Might have been, too."

Cagy now, Wildew said, "That don't make sense."

Rick had talked too much. The old habit of speaking freely to Wildew was hard to break. "Dunno," he said. "Maybe it don't. I was going to say something else. Nan still needs a friend. You're here. I ain't. Don't sell her out."

"Don't make the mistake of trying to give me orders," Wildew murmured. "You should know that, too."

"I'm giving you that one," Rick said sharply. "You sell Nan out and I'll beat some teeth down your throat."

"Not me you won't." Wildew raised a hand in mock salute, grinning. "So long, Stupid."

Rick rode out of the yard, not looking back. Stupid! Well, maybe he was. Maybe any man was stupid who let a woman kick him around the way Nan had. She'd cut his heart out and played catch with it. It wouldn't happen again. Then he wondered if Nan was watching him ride away. Probably not. She hadn't cared one way or the other.

He stayed on the north side of the river until he was past the Dolan place. It was not likely that Fleming was still up there on the rim, but the old wariness was in him now. He could not forget for a moment that danger was a constant presence, not if he wanted to live. That was funny, he thought. He still wanted to live. Nan's perfidy had not changed that.

110

It was dusk when he reached Hatchet. He dismounted in front of the house, noticing the saddled horse tied to the hitch rack. He wondered about it as he walked up the muddy path. He carefully scraped his boots on the steps, crossed the porch, and knocked.

Curly Hale opened the door, scowling when he saw who it was. He said curtly, "Rawlins' gunslingers ain't welcome here. Vamose."

"I ain't working for Rawlins," Rick said. "I want to see Miss Spargo."

"She ain't home to you," Hale growled. "I told you to git."

Lola had recognized his voice. She pushed past Hale who tried to block the doorway, and her voice was warmly eager when she asked, "Did you say you weren't working for Rawlins?"

She was wearing a maroon robe and slippers; her hair hung down her back in a dark mass that was loosely tied back of her neck with a small, red ribbon. He looked at her, feeling her vibrant personality and appreciating her mature beauty, and it struck him with stunning impact that those thoughts should not be in the mind of a man who had just been sent away by the girl he had considered himself engaged to.

"That's right," Rick said. "I came to take the job you offered me this afternoon if it's still open."

"Job," Hale bawled. "Now that's the damnedest thing I ever heard. Mister, you ain't getting no job on Hatchet."

"Hatchet may not belong to me very much longer," Lola said sharply, "but it does now and I'm still giving the orders. Get out of the way so he can come in."

Hale stared at Lola, his face red. "You don't know nothing about this hairpin."

111

"I'm not inquiring about his past history," Lola said coldly: "I'm judging him by what he did in town. He's hired. I don't know what he expects for wages, but whatever it is, he'll get it."

Hale stepped back into the room, big hands fisted at his sides. "What kind of a job do you figure to put him at?"

"Gunfighting. That's his trade and it's the kind of a job I'm going to need someone for."

Hale threw out a hand in savage protest. "I've stood by Hatchet when Vance done things I didn't like. He fired our old hands and took on a tough crew because Kinnear talked him into it, but they was cowhands. I'll say that for 'em. Malone's a gunslinger. I don't reckon he ever done a day's work in his life."

"I'm not one to make trouble," Rick said. "If I ain't welcome . . ."

"You're more than welcome," Lola cut in. "What's more, you're needed. Curly you aren't thinking straight. You'll be gone a day, maybe more. Now what will happen if you make the deal?"

"We'll round up as many steers as they'll take and we'll get 'em on the trail. Why?"

"And Joe Kinnear will have a fit when he finds out what's up. Are you big enough to keep your crew in line when Kinnear tells them not to move any stock?"

Hale's face was stormy, but her question brought a problem to his mind that apparently had not been there before. He backed away, scowling as he considered it.

"You figure Malone can whip 'em into line?" Hale asked.

"You know your men," Lola said curtly. "You can answer that question better than I can. If they don't work, you'll have to hire another crew. Joe will do everything he can to keep us from raising our interest."

"You're the boss," Hale said glumly, glaring at Rick. "Where are you gonna sleep?"

"In the bunkhouse, I reckon."

"He'll sleep in Vance's room," Lola said. "That's another thing. I'm afraid to stay here alone. I'll be safe with him in the house."

Hale threw up his hands. "Lola, haven't you had enough gossip spread about you? Don't you know what they'll say? . . ."

"I don't care. I'm past caring. I'm fighting. There are some things I can't do, but if I get the help I need, I'll lick them. That's all I care about."

Hale walked over to the table and picked up his Stetson. "I'll get along. Be back tomorrow night, I reckon." He tramped to the door and stopped, suspicious eyes on Rick. "If anything happens to Lola while I'm gone . . ."

"It won't," Rick said, "but something's gonna happen to you if you keep gabbing."

"I'm just warning you," Hale said, and went on past Rick to his horse.

Rick stood motionless until Hale had mounted and disappeared into the purple twilight. Then Lola asked, "Had supper?"

"No."

"Put your horses away," she said, "and then come in. I'll fix something."

# CHAPTER 11

## Man and Woman

IT WAS FULLY DARK WHEN RICK RETURNED TO THE
house. Lola had left a lamp in the front room. Hearing
Rick, she called, "I'm in the kitchen."

Rick glanced around the room, thinking that this was
the way Vance Spargo had left it. He had seen similar
rooms in a dozen ranch houses where there were no
women. It would not be long, he thought, for Lola to
make her impression upon it. He wondered how it had
been when she had lived here. Probably the same as it
was now, for Vance Spargo had not been the kind of
man who would have let his sister dominate him or
anything he owned. It had been his house and his ranch,
and it was unlikely that the thought had ever occurred to
him that it would ever be anything else.

Rick went on into the kitchen. Lola had set a place at
the table for him, and was at the stove frying ham and
potatoes. She said, "I haven't been home very long, so
there isn't much to eat. Curly brought some things from
town, but I didn't know what I needed and he didn't,
either. He's been at the cow camp."

She poured coffee and took the pot back to the stove.
Rick dropped into a chair and rolled a smoke, perfectly
relaxed for the first time in hours. Then it struck him
that he had no right to be, and he wondered about it.

He watched her bring a plate of biscuits to the table
and go back to the stove for the platter of ham and
potatoes, moving swiftly with the flowing rhythm of a
naturally graceful woman. While he ate, she opened a

114

can of peaches, emptied it into a dish, and placed it before him, then sat down on the opposite side of the table.

"What happened that Rawlins let you go?" she asked. When he hesitated, she added quickly, "Don't tell me if it's something you'd rather not talk about."

"It's kind of touchy," he said evasively, and went on eating.

She watched him, smiling a little as if this moment of intimacy were natural and desirable. When he was done, she said, "It's only fair to warn you that my chance of saving Hatchet is a mighty slim one, even with your help. It would be easier if I went back to The Dalles and let Tebo have Hatchet. I'd be rid of Kinnear that way."

Rick scooted back his chair and rolled a smoke. "Long odds don't scare me if that's what you're getting at. If there's any chance, we'll play it out."

"I heard that you and Wildew were partners," she said. "Did he stay on the Bent R?"

"He's there now, but I don't reckon he'll stay." Rick pulled on his cigarette for a moment, then added, "we wasn't exactly partners. Riding with him just got to be a sort of habit."

She was silent, her hands clasped on her lap, eyes on him. Suddenly he felt the need to talk and she seemed interested. He told her how it had been, drifting around after his mother had died and Wildew saving his life in Dodge City, and about the years since then, hiring out their guns and fighting for other men and the dissatisfaction that had steadily grown in him.

"There's a lot of things I don't savvy," he said. "Mom was good. She used to read the Bible to me. We were poor, but she kept me in school till she died. She used to talk about what was right and what was wrong, and

115

about not doing the things I'd be ashamed of later on. I got mighty tired of her preaching. Just let it go in one ear and out the other. I heard about men like Wildew. Thought I wanted to be like them. I started riding with him and for a while I worshiped him."

He stopped, frowning, his mind going back over the years, searching for the answer to the question that had bothered him for so long and found that it still eluded him.

"But you aren't like him," Lola said. "I don't think you ever will be."

"No. That's what I don't savvy. I mean, the older I got, the more I thought about how I wasn't getting anywhere. It never bothered Matt, but I got to thinking that if somebody plugged me, there was nobody on God's earth who'd give a damn. They'd bury me and put up a marker and that'd be the end of Rick Malone."

"I don't think it's hard to understand," she said. "The things your mother taught you when you were a boy made more impression on you than you realized. You aren't the kind of man who will let other people shape you into the sort of person they are. Vance was. Folks thought he was big and powerful, but he was weak. Inside, I mean. If he hadn't been, Kinnear would never have influenced him the way he did."

"Yeah, I reckon it took time for me to grow up." He thought of Nan who was still a girl, almost a child compared to Lola. Nan would change with time, too, and there might come a day when she would regret the decision she had made this afternoon, but it would be too late to change it. He added, "Sort of came to a head after me and Wildew got to the Bent R. I thought I was in love with Nan. She said she was in love with me, but today I found out different."

He wasn't sure, looking at Lola, whether she was surprised by what he said or not. She nodded as if understanding. "Nan's a nice girl. She'd make you a good wife."

"She won't make me any kind of a wife," he said bitterly. "Lou blew up when I told him. Nan and me figured he would, and she said she'd go with me. Said she'd seen women wait for their men and get old. I thought she meant it, but today she turned me down. Had to stick to Lou, she claimed, and all the time she knows he's crazy as a loon with his big talk about bringing the Bent R back and grabbing your range."

"There are different kinds of love," she said. "Nan had one kind of love for her grandfather and another for you. Had you thought of that?"

"Sure, but if a woman loves her kin more than the man she's going to marry, why, she don't love the man enough to make him a good wife."

"I'd hate to make that choice," she said slowly. "I loved Vance, you know. I was ashamed of him and I hated some of the things he did, but I still loved him."

"Me and Nan are finished," he said roughly. "Maybe Grant Jenner's her kind of man. She keeps saying he ain't, but maybe that's because Lou has done his damnedest to throw 'em together. She says she won't be bargained over."

"I know how she feels," Lola said.

"Well, she can have Jenner." He rose, suddenly filled with restlessness. "Guess I'll go to bed."

"I'll go, too. The dishes can wait till morning." She got up and walking to the back door, dropped a heavy bar across it. "You don't know how much better I feel with you here. I guess that if anybody wanted to break in, it would take more than a bar to keep them out."

"Kinnear?"

She nodded. "I'm scared, Rick, right down to my toes." She picked up the lamp and going into the front room, set it on the oak table and barred the front door. Turning, she smiled at him, trying to hide the fear that was in her. "I wish he knew you were here. Then he'd let me alone."

"I'd better sleep down here. If anybody tried to get in . . ."

"I want you up there across the hall from me." She picked up the lamp again, nodding at the one still on the table. "That's yours. Come on."

He followed her up the stairs, a strange uneasiness in him. Hale had been right about the gossip, and Lola was too fine to be hurt by it. She would not be defying it this way if circumstances had not forced her into a position where she felt that she was utterly helpless.

She stopped in the hall and opened a door to a bedroom. "This was Vance's room. It's yours now." She lifted her eyes to his, frowning. "I have a terrible feeling that I'm wrong. I'm putting you and Curly into more danger than I have any right to. Tebo, too. Kinnear would ruin him if he knew Tebo had promised me more time. Maybe I'm just stubborn in trying to hold Hatchet."

"It's more than keeping Hatchet." He went into the room and put the lamp down on the marble-topped bureau. Turning to her, he said, "You're not wrong. I'm remembering what you said about folks taking orders and letting Kinnear run everything. Well, we ain't taking his orders."

"We." She repeated the word softly as if liking it and wanting him to see that she did. "Rick, you'll never know how much you've done for me tonight."

118

"I ain't done nothing yet."

"Yes you have. When I heard what Fleming said, I wanted to curl up and die. Then after what you did, I came alive again." She swallowed. "I'm used to selfish men who never do anything unless they get paid for it. Oh, I can't say what I want to. Maybe I can show you, sometime."

She whirled and crossed the hall to her room. He heard her close her door. He started to shut his and decided against it. He was a sound sleeper. Something might happen tonight, and he could not take the risk of sleeping through it.

He jerked off his gun belt and threw it on the bed, then pulled off his boots. The room was quite bare, a man's room with just a bureau, a bed, and one chair. For a long time he sat there, thinking of Vance Spargo's death and how it had changed everything in Chinook County. It was like turning a pack of wolves loose on the valley.

He got up and began walking around the room, knowing he could not sleep if he went to bed. He was able to think of Nan now with cool detachment. It was just an incident in a lifetime. He could not let it be anything else. He had lost her; he had to accept that fact without worrying about it. It was too late to go back.

Love, it seemed to Rick, was something which must be returned. He could not love a woman who did not love him. It seemed simple now as he looked back on what had happened. Nan had been starved for affection and he had been handy. It must have been the same with him.

He sat down on the bed and rolled a smoke, his mind turning to Lola's trouble. There was a lot to be done and not much time. She had been honest with him in every way. She had no illusions about her chances, but she had courage. She'd fight it through to the finish.

He lost all sense of time. Slowly his mind, focused so closely on the woman who was sleeping across the hall from him, found the answer to her problem if she was willing to take his way out. He was nothing; he never had been anything, but with her help, he could put all of his past behind him.

He heard Lola's door open. He turned as she came into his room, worried eyes on him. She said, "I couldn't sleep and I heard you pacing around. Is something wrong? I mean, we're alone and if you're thinking about Nan . . ."

"No." He said the word sharply, more sharply than he intended to. "I've been thinking. That's all. I know what to do, but I ain't sure you'll do it. Sounds crazy . . ."

He stopped. It was crazy. He had met her only this afternoon. She didn't know anything about him. To her he was just another gunslinger like Matt Wildew who had taken a job.

She laughed softly. "Rick, if you know what to do, you've got to tell me. I don't, and I've racked my brain ever since I've got back."

She had put a robe on over her nightgown and her hair hung loosely down her back. He turned away. He knew what was wrong. She was expecting too much from him. He was a man filled with a man's passion, and she was the most attractive woman he had ever met. What did she think he was made of? Why in hell couldn't she stay in her bedroom and lock the door on him?

She came to him, touching his arm hesitantly. "What is it Rick?"

He wheeled and took her hands. He said savagely,

"Look. We're both crazy, me for wanting you and you for trusting me."

She was not offended and she did not draw back. She breathed, "Rick, if I told you what I thought you were, you wouldn't believe me. You'd think I was crazy and indecent because I know that just this afternoon you left the girl you were in love with."

"Shouldn't have told you," he muttered. "All right, I'm just a kid who had a case of puppy love. Let's forget Nan. I was going to say that Kinnear wants to marry you. If you were out of his reach, he'd let you alone. Then you wouldn't have any more trouble."

She shook her head. "I don't think he'd ever let me alone. But I know what you're thinking. About the gossip and me having you here in the house with me. All right, Rick. Think what you want to, I guess I'm no better than they say I am. You've heard the old saying about if you have the name, you might as well have the game."

It took a moment for him to understand what she was saying. There was none of the subterfuge about her that characterized so many women, none of the slyness and the trickery. Even in this she was straightforward and direct.

He put his arms around her and she lifted her face to his kiss. It was not like any kiss Nan had ever given him. It shocked him; it sent a hot flame burning through him. He felt the softness of her breasts against his chest, his hands were hard against her slim back, and her lips were warm and clinging. When he let her go and drew away, her face was still turned up to his and she let him see the hunger that was in her for him.

"Rick, I don't know what you're thinking about me, but . . ."

121

Someone pounded on the front door, the hard hammering blows of an angry man. Lola whirled and started out of the room. He caught up with her and grabbed her arm, held her. He said. "I'll see who it is. Stay here."

She hesitated, her face pale. Rick picked up his gun belt and buckled it around him, then Kinnear's great voice reached them, "Open up, Lola. Let me in, or I'll kick this damned door down."

# CHAPTER 12

## The Deserter

MATT WILDEW REMAINED MOTIONLESS BESIDE THE corral and watched Rick ride off, squinting against the slanting light of the dying sun. Usually he could face any situation with cool indifference, but now he was filled with a sense of outrage. He had spent six years of training Rick Malone; he had saved the boy's life more than once; he had insisted that any potential employer who wanted him had to take Rick, too.

The fact that everything Wildew had ever done for Rick had been prompted by motives that were entirely selfish did not enter his mind now. All he could think of was this one fact; Rick had ridden away, breaking off everything that had been between them, and then had added injury to insult by threatening to beat his teeth down his throat.

Then Wildew laughed. It was all right. Rick was not capable of changing. There was a better than even chance that if they had stayed together, the boy would turn out to be a liability. There were some things he couldn't learn, and now Wildew was convinced that if six years had not been long enough for him to learn them, another six wouldn't be, either.

Wildew remained there at the corral for a time, thinking about what Rick had said. Lola Spargo suspected Kinnear of murdering her brother. He might have done it, Wildew thought. The usual standards that governed a man's conduct would not apply to Kinnear. Wildew did not have the slightest doubt that if it would profit Kinnear, he would not have hesitated to shoot his best friend in the back.

Wildew smoked a cigarette, his sharp mind considering another thing Rick had said. The Spargo woman thought Kinnear had put Fleming up to saying what he had about her so that she would hear it. That, too, was something no ordinary man would have done, but Kinnear was capable of using any weapon he could lay his hands on to humble Lola Spargo.

Whether the gossip about her was true was not important. It was of long standing. Lola knew about it, and she would be hurt if it was fanned into life again. She would not be able to stay here, alone and friendless, and face it.

There was one more fact inherent in this situation. If Fleming had been carrying out Kinnear's orders, Fleming must be working for Kinnear. That meant Deke Cardigan had been taking Kinnear's pay, too, so now Kinnear would need another man. Fleming was of little value by himself. He wasn't smart, and he was only average with his gun.

Now Wildew's mind found the answer he had been groping for from the moment he had heard of Spargo's death. Kinnear could be made to pay big if the job was guaranteed. He had too much at stake to take the risk of losing now. The possibility of making the big stake was here before him, and there would be no splitting with Rick.

Quickly Wildew walked into the bunkhouse and packed up. He saddled his horse and loaded his pack horse. Tying them beside Jenner's mount, he went into the house. He had no qualms about what he planned to do. He had never quit an employer before when the man still needed him, but this was different. Before it had always paid him to stay on. In this case it would pay him to quit.

Rawlins and Jenner were still sitting at the table. Nan stood at the stove, her back to him. Hearing Wildew come in, she turned, saw who it was, and whirled back to the stove.

"Rick won't be back," Wildew said brutally. "He's hiring out to Lola Spargo."

"That bitch," Rawlins said as if it proved what he had been saying. "You hear, Nan?"

She didn't answer. Jenner got up, his eyes on the girl, and then sat down again, his usually cheerful face very grave. For a moment Wildew stood there, watching them and grinning. An occasion like this always made him feel more superior than he ordinarily did. Fools like these let their feelings control them. A smart man never did. Matt Wildew always controlled his feelings.

"I'll take my time," Wildew said.

Rawlins got up. It was the second time within the hour that he was too shocked to think coherently. He stared at Wildew, faded blue eyes wide and glassy.

Nan said, "Pay him and get rid of him. We're better off without him."Apparently Rawlins did not hear her. He started around the table, his gnarled hands

124

fisted. He said, his voice shaky, "I still need you. You can't quit me now."

"Never count on men like me and Rick," Wildew said carelessly. "You've got to do a job yourself if you want to have it done right." He motioned toward Jenner. "Don't count on hombres like him, neither. They say you used to be the big gun on this range. How'd you get there? By yourself, wasn't it? All right. If you ever get back up there, you'll do it yourself."

"I will," Rawlins shouted. "You're damned right I will. You're scared, ain't you? You figure I'm licked and you're running out because you're scared of Kinnear."

Wildew's face turned ugly. "Don't talk that way to me, old man. Gimme my dinero and I'll ride out."

"Pay him," Nan cried. "Just get rid of him."

"That's right," Wildew said. "Pay me and get rid of me. Rick was fool enough to pull out and leave you owing him, but not me"

"So you ain't scared," Rawlins muttered. "Then why are you pulling out when I still need you?" Impatient now, Wildew said the first thing that entered his mind. "You fired Rick. Don't reckon I want to stay on here by myself."

Still Rawlins stood motionless, blinking as if he were too dazed to think straight. Nan went to him and put her arms around him. She said, "Pay him, Grandpa. Just get him off the Bent R. You don't want a man you can't count on."

"No." Rawlins dug into his pocket. "No, I don't."

He threw fifty dollars in gold on the table, the coins

125

giving out a clear metallic ring. Wildew said, "Another ten, old man."

"The month ain't out yet," Rawlins snapped. "Take it and git."

Wildew shook his head. "There ain't much left of the month. I earned a month's wages. Fighting man's wages, and that means another ten."

"I ain't got no more," Rawlins muttered.

"You'd have had a hell of a time paying us if we had stayed on, now wouldn't you?" Wildew laughed. "Well, it'll square it if I take one of your horses."

"Here." Jenner threw another gold eagle on the table that rolled halfway across it and came to a stop beside the other coins. "Now will you slope out of here?"

Shrugging, Wildew picked up the money and put it in his pocket. As he walked to the door, Rawlins made a savage motion. "Keep going, Wildew, you and Malone. Just keep riding till you're plumb out of the county. You hear?"

Wildew raised a hand in a mocking gesture of farewell. "You never was big enough to give me an order I didn't want to take. It's gonna be fun, watching 'em pull you down off your high horse."

Wildew walked out, leaving Rawlins trembling with anger. Mounting, Wildew took the road to town. When he came opposite the Hatchet buildings, he reined up, wondering if Rick was there. He'd had some doubt about Rick working for the Spargo woman, although there had been no reason for him to lie about it.

Now, in the thin light, he could make out three horses racked in front of the house. He considered the possible implications of this. Perhaps Kinnear was here. If he had run into Rick, Kinnear would need help. It would be one way to start working for the lawyer, although

126

another plan had shaped itself in Wildew's mind that held far more promise.

He was still there when a man stalked out of the house, mounted, and rode down the lane. Wildew pulled back into the willows, and when the horseman reached the road, he saw that it was Curley Hale, Hatchet's ramrod. The crew had probably gone back to the cow camp. This might mean, then, that Rick and the Spargo woman were alone in the house, a piece of news that Kinnear would find interesting.

Wildew had assumed Hale was on his way to town. Instead the Hatchet man rode into the willows not more than twenty yards downstream from where Wildew sat his saddle, splashed across the river, and went on, riding north at a brisk pace. Wildew reined toward town, smiling. This, too, would interest Kinnear.

It was dark when Wildew left his horses in the livery stable. He took a room in the hotel and leaving his bedroll there, went back downstairs to the dining room and ate supper. He went outside and for a moment lingered on the boardwalk, considering the time element. In some ways it might be smart to wait until morning and see Kinnear in his office over the bank, then Wildew decided not to wait. He thought Kinnear would like what he had to propose, and if he did, he would not want to postpone action.

The town was very quiet, a fact that Wildew found amusing. These people didn't know it, but the quiet wouldn't last long. When the blow-up came, it would rock all of them back on their heels from Prine Tebo on down to the saloon swamper.

Wildew was still standing there when Cord Graham cruised by. He saw Wildew, recognized him and stopped, his weathered face shadowed by worry. He asked, "What the hell are you doing in town?"

"Rode in for supper," Wildew said evasively.

"Ain't Nan's cooking good enough for you no more?"

"Not now it ain't. I quit Rawlins."

It took a moment for Graham to digest that, his gaze not leaving Wildew's inscrutable face. He asked, "What about Malone?"

"Rawlins fired him."

"You're lying," Graham snorted. "Lou ain't one to get religion, and until he does, he'll be needing both of you."

"Don't call me a liar, Cord," Wildew said, his voice very mild. "I've got nothing against you. If you're smart, you'll leave it that way."

"All right, all right," Graham said hastily. "But I sure don't savvy. Why did Lou fire Malone?"

"Ask him. Say, have you seen Kinnear?"

"What business have you got with Kinnear?"

"You're a nosy old devil," Wildew said, and walked away, leaving the sheriff staring after him.

Kinnear's house was one block east of Main Street. It was not the biggest place in Bald Rock, but it was the newest and most expensive, and he had furnished it with a garish elegance that set it apart from the other dwellings in Bald Rock.

Wildew paused in front of the white picket fence, considering how to approach the lawyer. He had to say the right thing at the right time, or he'd fail before he had a chance to tell Kinnear what he had in mind. There was a light in the front of the house, and as Wildew opened the gate and moved up the walk, he realized that a tension had worked into him, a feeling which was unusual with him.

Wildew's knock brought Kinnear to the door. He frowned, staring at Wildew who stood in the shadows, his tall, broad-shouldered body making a strong shape against the lamplight. Wildew said, "You alone, Kinnear?"

The lawyer did not recognize him until he spoke. He said angrily, "I have no business with you. . . ."

Wildew stepped forward. "You're wrong, friend. With Cardigan beefed, you're needing another good man. I'm him. Fleming ain't worth a damn by himself."

The effrontery of it shocked Kinnear. He said, "If Lou Rawlins thinks he can . . ."

"Rawlins ain't got nothing to do with it. He's broke. I won't work for a man who can't pay me."

Kinnear stepped back to shut the door. Wildew jumped forward and put a shoulder against it. He said, "I figured you for a smart hombre, Kinnear. I've got news. If you're smart, you'll listen to me."

Kinnear hesitated, interest working into his bruised face. He said, "Let's hear it."

"If I ain't good enough to be invited into your house, friend," Wildew said, "you ain't good enough for me to work for."

Kinnear said, "Come in," and shut the door behind Wildew the instant he was through it.

"You're a friendly son," Wildew murmured, and crossed the hall into the living room.

Kinnear followed, hands shoved into his coat pockets. He said, his voice hostile, "Sit down."

"Take your fists out of your pockets," Wildew said irritably. "I didn't come here to get a slug in my guts."

Still Kinnear stood motionless, uneasy eyes on Wildew who was coolly glancing around at the expensive leather covered couch and chair, the

129

mahogany table, the great stone fireplace that took up most of the north wall of the room, and the painting of Mount Hood in the ornate frame, the only picture on the wall.

Resentment rose in him. Kinnear had everything anyone could want, yet he was no better than any other man with careless morals. He worked under cover; he used weaker men to gain his ends, but he was still a thief, and as far as Wildew was concerned, he merited no more respect than a common road agent.

"Quite a house, friend," Wildew murmured. "The law business must pay you pretty well."

"State your business and your price," Kinnear said coldly. "I'll be the judge of whether it's a good deal for me or not."

"And after you hear what I've got to say, you'll judge it ain't. Well, Kinnear, it ain't quite that simple. You need me more than the news I've got." Wildew walked around the table, his small smile fixed on the corners of his mouth. "Has the Spargo woman seen this room since she got back?"

Kinnear blew up. He cursed Wildew in a low, bitter tone, his face dark with savage fury. Wildew broke in, "You can stop right there, lawyer. It's my guess that you wouldn't have her in your house after you hear what I've got to say. Besides, you ain't God, sitting on a fat cloud, so high and mighty you can boot me into hell."

Kinnear dropped onto the leather couch, and when he had control of himself, he said, "Sit down, Wildew."

"That's better, friend, a lot better." Wildew walked across the room to a rocking chair and sat down. "I've got you pegged, Kinnear. I don't know how you got your money, but it was crooked enough, I reckon. Well, it ain't important. You've got plenty and you're going to

130

pay me. Big money. Savvy?"

"If you've got information . . ."

"It's more'n that. A lot more. I'll do the job Cardigan wasn't fast enough or smart enough to do. You're playing for big stakes. Without me, you're bound to lose. If you take my deal, you'll win. I guarantee it, or no pay."

Kinnear, Wildew knew, would not intend to pay him anything no matter whether he agreed to it or not. But he would pay. Kinnear was watching him intently, a hand coming up to his face and stroking his jet-black mustache.

"You'll guarantee what?" Kinnear asked finally.

"I'm a smart man," Wildew said. "I've been on this range long enough to hear some talk and put it together, so I know what you're working for. It's no secret, I reckon. A purty wife with a ranch. A political job. Very nice if you get 'em, Kinnear, but before you do, you've got to kick some people in the teeth. Now I'll fix it up for ten thousand dollars."

Kinnear laughed harshly. "Of all the damned gall . . ."

"You bet I've got gall, but that don't make no never mind. You're too smart to turn down the best deal you ever had offered you. If you do, there's one man who'll lick you."

"Who?"

"Rick Malone."

Kinnear snorted in derision. "If you think a gunslinging kid . . ."

"Sure, sure," Wildew broke in, "but he's more'n that. He's one of these crazy fools you can't buy. Don't ask me why. I've spent six years trying to poke some sense down his throat, but the older he got the harder he was to handle. Now he's gone to work for the Spargo

131

woman. . . ."

Kinnear jumped up. "What's that?"

"Rawlins fired him tonight and he's with the Spargo woman." Wildew reached for the makings, watching Kinnear's face. "They're alone. Curly Hale rode out tonight, heading north. Figure it out for yourself, friend."

Kinnear dropped back onto the couch as if his knees would not hold him. "You sure?"

"I saw Hale leave. He rode like he was going somewhere. Now I think the Spargo woman will like Rick pretty well, and she can pick him up on the bounce. He figured he was in love with Nan Rawlins, but she turned him down when it came to leaving Lou. Nothing like another woman's arms when a man's just lost the one he wanted."

Kinnear threw out a hand in a violent gesture. "I don't believe it. You're lying."

"Suppose me'n you ride out there."

Kinnear hunched forward, his meaty shoulders slack, and for the first time since Wildew had come to Chinook County, he saw that the man's confidence was shaken. He was afraid, Wildew thought, to accept the challenge.

Wildew rolled his smoke and fired it, waiting. There was no sound in the room for a long moment except Kinnear's heavy breathing and the ticking of the clock that hung on the wall above the fireplace. Then Kinnear said slowly, "All right, we'll go out there. If you're lying to me . . ."

"Don't waste none of your tough talk on me," Wildew broke in irritably. "Save it for Malone. He's handy, Kinnear. You found out how handy he was with his fists and you saw him down Cardigan. He's smart, too. I never was much of a gambler, but I'd give odds on him licking you unless I'm siding you."

"I don't savvy," Kinnear said slowly. "You and Malone were partners and you're supposed to be a man whose word is good. Now you're double-crossing Malone."

"I'm smarter'n he is. We busted up." Wildew sucked in a lungful of smoke and let it out slowly, waiting for Kinnear to digest that. Then he added, "I'll tell you how it is, lawyer. I'm getting too old for this business. I've got to make my stake and get out, or I'll wind up with my belly full of lead. You're gonna give me that stake."

This was talk Kinnear could understand. He asked, "What have you got to offer that's worth ten thousand?"

"Before I tell you that, I want to know where Fleming is."

"Why?"

"He tried to drygulch Malone and missed. Malone says he'll hang around here long enough to get you and Fleming. Now I've got it all figured out, but I need Fleming."

Kinnear thought about that for a moment. Then he said reluctantly, "He's holed up in the Dolan house."

Wildew nodded. "That's fine. We'll light out for Hatchet and you can see if Malone's there. Then we'll find Fleming. Just one thing, Kinnear. If you try to cheat me, I'll kill you. I think you know that."

"Nobody threatens me . . ." Kinnear began belligerently.

"I ain't threatening you. I'm just telling you how it'll be." Wildew rubbed out his cigarette. "You don't like me, Kinnear. That's fair enough because I sure as hell don't like you. You're a back-shooting killer. The way I figure, that makes you low enough to walk under a

133

sidewinder's belly with your fancy Stetson on."

Kinnear froze. "What do you mean, calling me a back-shooting killer?"

"Spargo. That's who I mean."

"He was my friend. Why in hell would I kill him?"

"Dunno, but Lola Spargo thinks you done it. That's why she and Malone will make a tough team if they get together. Let's put it this way. You want the Spargo woman and you want Hatchet. Likewise you want Rawlins out of the way because he's kicking dust into your face. When you get Hatchet, you want the range all the way up to the head of Pine River. With Rawlins dead, Jenner wouldn't be no bother. That right?"

"You're talking," Kinnear said sullenly.

"Now I want a straight answer. Are we making a deal or not?"

"All right," Kinnear said, "but you've got to understand I'm staying out of it."

Wildew grinned. "Your kind always does. Now I'll tell you how we'll work it. After you leave Hatchet, I'll get Malone out of the house and take him to the old Dolan place. I'll hold him there while Fleming plugs Rawlins. Then we'll pin the killing on Malone. Nan and Jenner will testify that he had a hell of a row with Rawlins before he left the Bent R. With Graham sheriff and you the district attorney, you ought to be able to nail him for Spargo's killing, too, before you're done with him."

It appealed to Kinnear. He got up and began pacing around the room, frowning as he considered this. The plan, Wildew thought, was foolproof if Fleming took care of his part. Shooting a man from ambush was something he could and would do for a price.

"Soon as you get the ten thousand, you'll clear out of

134

the county and stay out?" Kinnear asked.

"I'll burn the breeze getting out," Wildew said, "unless you want me to testify about the ruckus Malone had with Rawlins."

"That won't be necessary."

"And don't overlook the fact that with Malone gone and Tebo putting the pressure on the Spargo woman, she'll cave. She'll be damned glad to marry you."

"Leave her out of it," Kinnear said sharply. "Get your horse. I'll meet you on the road east of town."

Wildew rose. "I'll be along."

He walked rapidly back to the stable and saddled his horse. He had no illusions about Kinnear's sense of honor. Even if everything went as they had planned, Kinnear would laugh in his face when it came time to collect the ten thousand, but he wouldn't laugh long, not with the muzzle of Wildew's gun in front of his belly. There might be trouble after he was paid, but Wildew was not a man to worry about that kind of trouble. Once he had the money, he'd be hard to find.

He left town, riding back toward Hatchet, and met Kinnear on the road a mile east of Bald Rock. They went on together, saying nothing. When they reached the lane that led to the Hatchet buildings, Wildew saw that there was a light in an upstairs window of the house. He had supposed Lola and Rick would be in bed and asleep.

"Wait," Wildew said, and reined up. "Somebody's awake."

"It doesn't make any difference," Kinnear snapped. "I'll see if Malone's there. If he ain't, I'll know you're lying and the deal's off."

"Want to take a look in the corral for his horses?"

"No."

135

"You gonna tackle him alone, or you want me to trail along?"

"You stay here. You'll have a hell of a time getting him out of the house if he knows you're working for me."

"I thought maybe you was afraid of him."

"Not any," Kinnear snapped. "Won't take me long if he's in the house."

Kinnear rode up the lane and disappeared in the darkness. Wildew sat his saddle, smiling, thoroughly satisfied with the way this had gone. The only danger was that Kinnear might lose his head and try for his gun. If he did, he'd be a dead man, but he probably knew it, so it wasn't likely he'd try.

Wildew rolled and fired a cigarette, cupping the match flame with a hand so it could not be seen from the house. He waited there at the head of the lane, putting his mind to the problem of getting Rick out of the house. Presently it came to him how it could be done.

# CHAPTER 13

### Prisoner

FOR A MOMENT RICK AND LOLA STOOD MOTIONLESS after they recognized Kinnear's voice, then Lola whispered, "What do you suppose he wants?"

"I'll find out." Rick picked up the lamp and stepped into the hall. "Stay here. I'll talk to him."

He went down the stairs and set the lamp on the table. Lifting the bar, he opened the door, right hand on gun butt, but he saw at once that Kinnear was not looking for shooting trouble. The lawyer stood on the porch, glaring at Rick, a bitter angry man.

"What are you doing here, Malone?" Kinnear demanded.

"Working for Hatchet."

Kinnear came in, gaze swinging around the room, then he asked, "Where's Lola?"

"Upstairs."

"I want to see her."

"She don't want to see you. Let's get this straight, Kinnear. You ain't fooling anybody. It ain't Tebo who's after Hatchet. It's you. One of these days I'll be looking at you over a gun barrel. Might save trouble if we settled this right now."

Apparently Kinnear had not heard. He circled the room, a muscle in his cheek beating with the regularity of a pulse, then he saw his picture on the floor and turned to face Rick. "You tell Lola I want to see her, or I'll go up to her room."

"You won't make it past the first three steps."

Kinnear wheeled toward the stairs. "You won't shoot a man in the back," he said, and put a foot on the first step.

"Don't go any farther," Rick called, and drew his gun.

"Wait, Joe," Lola said, and came down the stairs to him.

Kinnear drew back, his eyes fixed on her pale face. She was worried and frightened, but there was something else on her face, the glory look of a woman who has just been kissed by the man she loved. Kinnear might have noticed it, or perhaps he was suspicious, finding her alone with Rick and dressed in a nightgown and robe, her dark hair down her back.

"Have you lost your mind, staying here with him?" Kinnear demanded.

"No."

"Where's Hale?"

"Gone."

"Where?"

"Hatchet business, Joe. I'm not as bad off as you tried to make me think last night. We're going to pull through."

Kinnear swung around to look at Rick who had dropped his gun back into leather. Then he gave his back to Rick again, visibly shaken and puzzled. "Why did you hire Malone?"

"I need him. I'll fight you with every weapon I can find, and a gun in Rick's hand is a very effective one."

"But you don't need it, Lola. I'll help you. I told you that last night. A gun won't change anything unless you plan to rob the bank."

"You aren't as tough as you were last night, Joe. Sure you'll help me, but how? On your terms, isn't it? I won't deal that way."

"Lola, I've asked you to marry me. I'm asking you once more. Now."

She said, "No."

"I'll never ask you again." He motioned toward Rick. "A man would have to love you to want to marry you after finding him here."

"A strange kind of love," she cried. "You'd destroy anything or anybody that you loved. I don't want any of it."

"You bitch," he breathed. "You man-hungry bitch."

Rick had held his temper under a tight rein, thinking that Lola would want to handle this, but now his control broke, and he lunged toward Kinnear, his hands

138

reaching for him. He would have killed the lawyer then, killed him with his hands, for in that wild, crazy instant all the teaching Wildew had given him about not losing his head was blotted out by the red curtain that fury drew across his mind.

Lola jumped between them, crying, "Rick! No, Rick! We'll give him time and we'll let him hang himself."

She backed up against Kinnear, facing Rick who stopped and wiped a hand across his face, the fury dying in him. He thought too much of Lola to settle with Kinnear in front of her. She had suffered enough without having to watch another killing.

"Get out." Rick motioned toward the door. "You can stop nagging her. She's going to marry me."

He saw Lola tremble, one hand coming up to clutch her throat; he watched Kinnear stalk to the door and he made a turn to keep his eyes on the lawyer, and when the man reached the door, he said, "I don't like the notion of being drygulched. I don't aim to live in this valley and run the chance of having you or Fleming take a shot at me every time I poke my head out of doors."

Kinnear kept on going. He didn't say anything; he did not look back. Rick waited until he heard the sound of Kinnear's horse galloping down the lane then he closed the door and barred it. When he turned, he saw that Lola had moved halfway across the room and stopped beside the table, one hand upon it as if her legs would not support her.

"So I'm marrying you," Lola breathed. "I may be deaf, but I didn't hear you propose."

"I figured the only way to get him off your neck is for you to marry someone else. I told you a while ago I knew what to do. I was going to ask you then to marry me, but I didn't get a chance."

She walked to the couch and sat down, her head against the wall as if utterly weary. "Have you forgotten about Nan?"

"She doesn't want me. She made that clear." He put a hand out toward her and then dropped it, sensing that he was going at this the wrong way. "I don't figure Nan has anything to do with me. I don't have no big ideas about being anything, but I want to amount to something."

"I know," she said in a low voice. "I guess all men do."

"Not the way I do." He sat down beside her. "Maybe it's just that I've got to the place where I'll change or go on like I was and I don't want to do that. I'll wind up being another Matt Wildew."

"You were in love with Nan," Lola breathed. "If you married me, you'd keep on thinking about her and wondering how big a mistake you had made."

"I never would." He took her hand. "This afternoon Tebo told me I could make a place for myself in this country. That's what I'd like to do. You can help me and I can help you."

"A deal," she said scornfully. "Just a business deal. It's no good, Rick. Just no good."

She began to cry. He felt a sudden burst of irritation. She was acting like a woman now, inconsistent and emotional. He had not thought she was that way. She was tackling a man's job and he had thought she would see this the way a man would, but now she sat with her head bowed, her shoulders shaking.

The irritation died in him. He couldn't blame her. She had been back only twenty-four hours. Too many things had happened in that time. He took her hands.

"Listen, Lola. It would be good for both of us. I found

140

out something when I kissed you. I said that what I wanted to do sounded crazy. It still does. We've known each other just a few hours. But everything seems kind of crazy. I can do a lot for you I can't if I'm just a hired hand. Let me have a chance. I won't hurry you. Maybe in time I can be the kind of man you could love."

She pulled her hands away from his and finding a handkerchief in the pocket of her robe, wiped her eyes. She said, "Vance hated crying women. I guess all men do, but I couldn't help it. It just seemed the wrong way for us to start."

"Think about it," he said. "If you don't want me, say so."

She rose and stood looking at him, her chin trembling.

"I can't say that, Rick. I'll try . . ."

A hard rap on the door brought Rick to his feet, hand instinctively reaching for his gun. He didn't draw it. He dropped his hand, glancing at Lola. It was a habit he had to break. Like Wildew, he had learned to think first of his gun when it came to settling any problem.

"I'll see who it is," Lola said.

"No." Rick stepped in front of her. "I've got a hunch this is my kind of business."

The knock came again, harder this time. Rick moved to the door, calling, "Who is it?"

"Matt. I'm supposed to fetch you back to the Bent R."

"I ain't going back," Rick shouted. "You oughtta know that."

"Damn it, open the door," Wildew shouted. "Old Lou just stopped a slug with his brisket."

Lola cried out involuntarily. Rick hesitated, uncertain what he should do. At the moment he felt no regret about Lou Rawlins' death. His feeling surprised him, for he had never been able to think of death in the cold, detached way Wildew did, but he was thinking of it that way now, and it worried him. Perhaps, as Tebo had suggested, some of Wildew's cussedness had rubbed off on him.

"Let him in," Lola said.

Rick lifted the bar and opened the door, standing to one side, right hand drawing his Colt from leather. He would never be able to trust Wildew again.

"Mighty slow," Wildew grumbled as he came in. "Put that iron up, damn it. I'm just an errand boy."

"How did it happen?" Lola asked.

"Bushwhacked. Shot through the window from outside."

"Who did it?" Lola asked.

"I wouldn't have a guess as to that, ma'am," Wildew said. "I was asleep in the bunkhouse. Seemed like Lou was fretting so much he hadn't even gone to bed. He was sitting there in his front room when somebody plugged him from outside. When I got into the house, Lou was dead and Nan was blubbering like she was crazy."

It was like Wildew to say it that way and again the sense of irritation crowded Rick. Wildew's cussedness had not rubbed off on him. Not much of it anyhow.

Rick said, "Nothing I can do."

"Nan wants you. I told her you wouldn't come, but she said you would."

"Get Jenner."

"I said something like that, and she bawled louder than ever. She wants you. Jenner wouldn't do."

"Tell her I ain't . . ."

"No, Rick." Lola was beside him, her hand on his arm. "You've got to go. I think you'll find out for sure while you're there how you feel about her."

"I know how I feel," he said bitterly. "It's over, I tell you."

"Please, Rick. She's in trouble. It's the only decent thing you can do."

She was right. He glanced at Wildew, knowing that he would see the man's cynical grin curling the corners of his mouth. It was there. He could guess what the gunman was thinking. Soft spot! Well, he had it and it would be in him until he died.

"All right, I'll go," Rick said, and went upstairs for his boots.

When he returned a moment later and picked up his hat from the table, he realized that Lola's eyes followed him as if haunted by the fear she would not see him again. He came to her and put his arms around her. She looked up at him, whispering, "Later, Rick, if you come back."

"I'll be back," he said. "Don't make no mistake about that."

He went out of the house, Wildew following, and when the door closed, the gunman said, "You're making real headway with her, kid. I didn't figure you were that smart."

Rick wheeled, his taut temper snapping. "Matt, I told you once I'd knock some teeth down your throat. You say that again and I'll do it."

"Don't be so damned ringy," Wildew said mildly. "I ain't blaming you. Not a little bit."

Rick strode on toward the corral. As he saddled his horse, he wondered who had killed Rawlins. The murder did not surprise him. Rawlins had made a pest out of himself today. Kinnear would have it easier with Rawlins out of the way. Graham, too. The sheriff could

143

lay Spargo's killing on him. That brought another thought to his mind that hit him with a jarring impact. It might have been Curly Hale, for Rawlins' threats had been directed at Hatchet.

Mounting, Rick joined Wildew who was waiting in the lane. As they rode away from Hatchet, the sense of uneasiness grew in Rick. Rawlins' killing did not seem like the kind of thing Hale would do, but at a time like this men did strange things they would not ordinarily do. That was another thing Wildew had taught him.

They reached the road and turned east, hoofs making a faint whisper of sound against the soaked earth. The sky was clear, stars burning with the sharp glitter that was characteristic of the high country. There was no moon, and as they rode, the valley narrowed until the rimrock crowded in against them, the black walls making two sharp lines against the sky.

They passed several deserted buildings. Hatchet range now, this land had once belonged to little men, and Rick remembered what Lola had said that afternoon about not being able to undo the things Vance had done. You could go ahead but there was no trail that led back into time. Now Lou Rawlins was dead, and indirectly Vance Spargo had brought it about. Perhaps that thought had been in Lola's mind when she had begged him to go to Nan.

"Lou cash in right off?" Rick asked.

"I reckon. The slug got him dead center."

"You look around?"

"Sure. A horse had been hitched out past the corral. Tracks didn't mean nothing. That's all I found."

They were silent, Rick's mind turning again to Hale. It probably wasn't him. Fleming? It seemed more like him than anyone else Rick could think of. They were almost to the Dolan place then, Jenner's Diamond J not far ahead. Rick wondered what Jenner would think now. He would not have Rawlins to lean against and tell him what to do. Jenner might be thankful for that.

Wildew's horse swung close to Rick. The gunman's hand darted out and lifted Rick's Colt. He said, his voice quite casual, "You know me well enough to be damned sure I wouldn't miss at this distance even in the dark. Pull up."

Rick reined his horse to a stop, too surprised to think coherently. He blurted, "What the hell are you pulling off?"

"Just a little scheme I thought up," Wildew said. "Get down. Leave your horse right here. I'll put him away when I get around to it."

Rick obeyed, knowing Wildew too well to take any crazy chance now. He swung out of the saddle, Wildew ordering, "Come around here. Slow like."

Again Rick obeyed. Then Wildew stepped down. He said, "Get into the house."

"Maybe you'd better tell me what this scheme of yours is."

"Not yet." Wildew laughed "I always said your soft spot would get you killed. Now I'd never jump into no bog hole like you done, but you didn't even suspicion that something was wrong."

Rick walked through the weeds of the yard. Wildew called, "Open up. I've got him."

The door swung open, Kinnear saying, "Good. Took you a little longer than I expected."

Rick went into the house, Wildew a pace behind him, gun muzzle a few inches from the small of Rick's back. Kinnear was there, a malicious expression of triumph on his battered face. Fleming was there, too, lips pulled

145

away from big teeth in an ugly grin.

"You need practice," Rick said to Fleming. "You done some poor shooting this afternoon."

"Shut up," Fleming shouted. "I'll start practicing on you right now if you open your mug about that again."

"Stop your gabbling," Kinnear said, exasperated. "You fizzled like a beginner today. Don't fizzle again."

"I won't," Fleming promised eagerly.

"Five hundred if you pull if off," Kinnear said. "Then get out of the country."

"Rawlins is as good as dead," Fleming said.

"Over there is the chair, kid," Wildew said. "Got that rope, Fleming?"

For a moment Rick hesitated, eyes touching each man briefly. Kinnear's right hand was in his pocket; Wildew still had his gun lined on Rick's belly. Fleming had wheeled to a corner and picked up a rope.

"I've got it," Fleming said. "Get him into that chair. I'll tie him so he'll stay tied."

"Matt, I'd think I was asleep and dreaming this . . ."

"Do what you're told," Wildew said softly.

There was no choice. They'd cut him down if he made a play now. He might have a chance later. He sat down and Fleming tied him, hands behind his back, ankles together, and then looped the rope tightly around his chest so that he was bound against the back of the chair. Then Fleming moved around him and looked down.

"Think I'll wait and watch 'em hang you," he said.

"Get moving. The sun will be up if you keep gabbing." Wildew jerked Rick's hat off his head and handed it to Fleming. "Leave it by the corral that's closest to the house."

Fleming took the hat with his left hand, then raised

146

his right and cracked Rick on the side of the head, a vicious blow that sent stars pinwheeling across his vision.

"You damned yellow belly." Wildew kicked Fleming hard in the seat. "Get out of here."

Fleming stumbled and almost fell before he regained his balance. He wheeled cursing Wildew, a fist cocked.

Kinnear said, "If you don't get out of here . . ."

"I'm going." Fleming dropped his fist and stalked to the door. Then he turned back. "Wildew, if you do that again . . ."

"Don't scare me," Wildew jeered.

"Fleming, so help me," Kinnear shouted, "I'll do this job myself if you don't want the five . . ."

Fleming went out, slamming the door behind him. Kinnear stood motionless until he heard Fleming ride away. Then he nodded at Wildew. "Put the horses in the shed. I'll wait here till you get back."

Wildew nodded and left the house. Kinnear walked around the room, frowning as if considering what lay ahead. Rick asked, "Rawlins ain't dead yet?"

"Not yet." Kinnear stopped and looked at Rick, stroking his mustache, very pleased with himself. "So you're marrying Lola, are you? Well Malone, I want to see that."

Rick said nothing. Kinnear began pacing again. Rick, looking around the room, saw that the windows were covered with blankets. Anyone riding by would not see the lamplight. It didn't make any difference. No one riding by would help him. He could not save Rawlins' life; it was probable he could not even save his own.

The room showed that no one had lived here for a long time. Dirt had blown in through a broken window, the wallpaper was torn off in long shreds, and there was

147

no furniture left except the chair Rick was bound to and a battered table. Mary Dolan had taken everything of value when she had moved to town.

Wildew came in. He said, "Better dust, Kinnear. You need to be in town before sunup."

"Graham will be out here before noon," Kinnear said.

After Kinnear left, Wildew stood looking down at Rick, his face grave. "Things change, don't they, kid? Now your soft spot is gonna kill you like I said. Want to know how?"

"You've told me about that soft spot enough times . . ."

"Yeah, reckon I have. Now I want to tell you how it'll kill you. At the end of a rope, Rick, and that's a hell of a way for a man to die."

# CHAPTER 14

## Murder at Dawn

IT WAS DUSK BY THE TIME NAN FINISHED THE SUPPER dishes. She could hear the low talk from the front room where Jenner and her grandfather had gone after they had finished eating. She could not make out what was said; she didn't care. At the moment nothing seemed important to her.

She left the house and walked around the woodshed and on to the timber where she had waited for Rick so many times. He would not come tonight. He would never come again. She leaned against the trunk of a pine, staring up at the tall sky, and for the first time in her life, it seemed distant and coldly hostile.

Darkness was moving in, the first stars beginning to

148

show with the pale silver of early evening. The cool air was damp and heavy with mountain smell. This was her world and she loved it; she could not think of living any where else. She wondered if that had had something to do with her turning Rick down.

It seemed to Nan that she both hated and loved her grandfather, although it seemed impossible to have such opposite emotions at the same time. Or perhaps she hated herself for the weakness she had shown when she had been forced to make a decision. Or had it been weakness?

She owed a great deal to her grandfather. It was Rick who was wrong. He could have waited. He could have gone away and come back when everything was settled. If he loved her, he would have done that. *If he loved her!*

She was too upset to think coherently. Now she sought refuge in the thought that Rick had never really loved her, but she was inherently honest, and it came to her that she could not be sure she had ever loved Rick.

Nan remembered the talk she'd had with Mary Dolan who had never doubted her feeling for Hank. It had not been that way with Nan. There was Grant. In spite of all she had said about him, she could not overlook the kindness that was in him, the constant loyalty. Grant put up with Lou's bossy, bullying ways because of her.

Nan seldom cried. She could not cry now. It would have been better if she could have. Tears would relieve the deep ache that was inside her. She had never felt this way before. Time might change things. No, it probably wouldn't. She'd feel this way forever. Rick was gone. Gone! She said the word aloud, realizing then she had been unconsciously listening for his footsteps as she had so many times, standing just as she was now under this

149

pine.

Then another thought came to her. She knew, and Rick had had the same conviction, that her grandfather was wrong. Any sane man Lou's age would have been satisfied to live life out here. There would be no trouble now that Vance Spargo was dead. They could get along, Lou and Grant. Let them put their places together. That was all right. It was the reaching out for something which was not theirs that was wrong.

Wrong or not, Lou Rawlins would not change. For some reason Nan wondered about her mother. She could not remember her. She had not known very many women. There had been few neighbors, and Mary was the only girl her own age among them. Then, after Hank had been killed and Mary had moved to town, Nan had been the only woman in the upper end of the valley.

Nan did remember her father, a mild man who had been much like Grant. He had bowed to Lou from force of habit, and Nan had the feeling that Lou's bullying had worn him down until he had not wanted to live. Now it had killed something in her. Then, with the memory of past injuries flooding her, she reached her decision. She would leave the Bent R if Lou did not give up his crazy project of fighting for Hatchet range.

She walked back to the house. It was completely dark except for the thin starshine, and she did not see Grant until she reached the back porch. He stood there, motionless, waiting for her. She stopped a step from him, trying to see his face, but to her eyes it was only a pale blob that seemed to be without expression.

"I've been looking for you," he said. "I had to talk to you."

"I'm glad," she said softly. "I'd feel better if I could talk to someone."

He sat on the steps and pulled her down beside him. He said, "There are a few things I've got to know. Lou swears he's heading out for the cow camp in the morning and all hell won't stop him. I've never quarreled with him. I've just tried to get along. Maybe I don't have no backbone. Just mush. That's what Malone thinks, ain't it?"

"Let's not talk about him."

"We've got to. If you love him, you don't love me and never will. I've got to hear it one more time. If you tell me now, I'll believe it. Then I'll go see Prine Tebo in the morning. He'll buy the Diamond J and I'll get out of the country and stay out."

She gripped his hand. "Don't do that, Grant. It's been your home for a long time. You'd never forgive yourself if you sold the Diamond J."

"Maybe not," he said somberly. "But I couldn't stay here and see you married to Malone and having his children and being happy with him. I'd rather be a thousand miles away."

"He'll never come back."

"I think that's up to you," he said. "He will if you want him, but I'm thinking you're young. Maybe you just thought you were in love with him. You've been alone so long, never seeing anybody but me and Lou and our crews."

"I've been alone too much all right," she said dully. "'Rick was new. He'd been to a lot of places. I—I liked him. I wasn't really fair, telling him I'd go away with him. I must have known I couldn't when the time came."

"You ain't answering my question," he said doggedly. "If you think you could ever love me, I'd go along with Lou just because he is your grandfather."

"No, Grant," she said. "We know he's wrong. Don't ruin yourself because of me."

"Maybe you keep thinking of me like I was your brother or something. That won't do for me. That's why I had to see you tonight. You've turned me down dozens of times. I kept coming back because I always believed that some time you'd change. Now I've got to know. I can't keep on coming back."

"Don't press me now," she whispered. "In the morning I'll know."

"If you don't know now, how will you know in the morning?" he asked bitterly.

He started to get up, but she pulled him back. "I made one decision tonight, Grant. You've got to make the same decision. If Grandpa goes ahead, I'm leaving. I'll go in and tell him now."

"He's gone to bed," Jenner said. "I don't think you can leave him, or you'd have gone with Malone."

"This is different. I won't leave him because of someone else. I'll do it to keep him from making a mistake that would ruin all of us."

Jenner was silent a moment, then he said, "I've thought about this till I'm about crazy. When Spargo told us last spring he was going to run us out, I was willing to fight. Now it's different, but Lou can't see it. He's crazy, Nan. That's the whole thing, crazy with thinking about how big he used to be. He won't quit trying till he's dead."

"Let me have tonight, Grant," she whispered. "I love you. Not the way I thought I loved Rick, but I love you. He was a stranger. It was kind of exciting just to have him around. Or maybe it was because I'd known you so long I didn't know how I felt. I just took you for granted."

"If you'll marry me," he said humbly, "I'll make you happy. I promise."

"Would you take me, knowing you had only part of my heart?"

"I'd take you any way I could get you," he said. "I love you that much."

It was all she could expect from him; it was more than she deserved. In time she could love him, really love him in the way he deserved. If there were just the two of them . . .! Somehow she had to push her grandfather far enough out of her life so that his shadow would not be between her and Grant. Her husband must be her man; he must be a free man.

"I don't know," she said miserably. "It still comes back to Grandpa. I guess anyone else would say he's made his bed and he can lie in it, but I'm a little silly. If he went away, I'd worry about him. Nobody to rub his back when he gets rheumatism. Nobody to cook the way he likes things. I'm the only one who knows how to do things for him."

"I'll be back at sunup," he said. "I've knuckled down to him too long, and I'm going to tell him so in the morning."

He rose, and this time she did not try to hold him. She said, "I'll tell him I'm leaving if he keeps on."

"Maybe it will stop him," Jenner said. "Good night."

"Good night, Grant," she said, and sat there until she heard him ride away.

She went into the house, and taking the lamp from the kitchen table, paused for a moment outside Lou's room. He was snoring with the regularity of a man who was sleeping soundly. Trouble had never kept him awake. She went on into her room, the certainty in her that it would make no difference to him what she or Grant

153

said. Lou Rawlins was driven by his stubborn will to the point where nothing in the world would change him.

She closed the door and set the lamp on the bureau. For a moment she stood looking around, thinking that this was the last night she would be here. She opened a bureau drawer and took out a tintype of her mother, a kindly-faced woman whom Nan had always been sure she would have loved if she'd had a chance.

She had studied the picture many times, thinking how much she had missed by not knowing her mother and wondering if she was like her. Nobody had ever said. Lou never talked about her. Nan had the impression that they hadn't got along. She put the tintype back and closed the drawer,

Her room! Not much furniture. Hardly even enough to call it "her room." Just the old scarred bureau and bed and a rocking chair. A bare room that she had tried to fix up with a few pieces of fancy work and a lace bedspread. She had wanted nice things, but when she'd mentioned it to Lou, he'd put her off with, "Can't afford it. If I had money to throw around for geegaws, I'd buy a good bull."

She lay down on the bed, still wearing her riding clothes she had put on that morning. She dozed fitfully, got up and blew out the lamp, but still did not sleep well. She realized with something of a shock that Rick was not in her thoughts. Her mind was on Grant and her grandfather, and she wondered if anyone else had ever been caught in a trap like this, a trap that offered no means of escape.

Suddenly she was aware that it was dawn. She heard Lou get up, grunting and yawning as he did every morning; she heard him start the fire and when the pine kindling was crackling in the kitchen range, he knocked on her door.

"Time to rise and shine," he shouted. "Grant's gonna eat with us and then we're lighting out for the cow camp."

"All right," she called, and lay motionless until his steps faded.

She rose, tired all the way through her slender body, so tired that she thought she could not stand the hours that lay ahead. She went into the kitchen and set the tea kettle on the front of the stove. Lou would be back in a few minutes, impatient with her because breakfast wasn't ready. She'd have it out with him then, once and for all, and afterwards she'd pack up and leave. Or could she do it? Would it be the same as it had been when Rick had forced her to make this same decision?

The crack of a rifle was as unexpected and shocking as thunder from a clear sky. It came again, the second shot, hard upon the echoes of the first. She grabbed a Winchester from the wall and ran out through the back door. In the pearl gray light she saw Lou lying halfway between the house and corrals; she glimpsed the blurred figure of a man running for his horse and she fired.

Nan was ordinarily a good shot, but she was trembling and the light was too thin for accurate shooting. She missed, levered another shell into the chamber and pulled trigger again. The man stumbled, regained his balance and reached his horse. She fired two more times, and then he was in the saddle and galloping away.

She dropped her rifle and ran to her grandfather. He was still breathing; blood was a scarlet froth on his lips, and she knew at once he was dying. She sat down beside him and took his head in her lap, thinking this couldn't have happened. It must be a nightmare. She

155

was still in bed; she was asleep.

Lou stirred and reached for her hand. His eyes were open, but he found it hard to talk. No, this was not a nightmare. She bent down. He breathed, "Dunno who got me. He was yonder by the corrals."

"I'll get you into the house. I'll go for the doctor. Grant will be along."

"No time. You'll be all right, you and Grant. The Bent R and the Diamond J."

Even now his last thought was about their ranches. He tried to say something, but strength had fled. He was staring at her, eyes blank in death, and a trickle of blood ran down his chin and on to his beard. She was still sitting there, there holding his head when Grant rode into the yard. He dismounted and knelt beside her.

"Dead?"

"Yes, he's dead," Nan breathed. "Somebody got him when he went out to water the horses."

"You see who it was?"

"No. I saw the man but I didn't know him. I shot, but he got away. I couldn't see very well, Grant. It wasn't light enough."

"Stay here," he said, and ran toward the corrals.

The sun was showing above the pine ridges to the east when he came back, walking slowly as if he could not tell her what he knew. He was carrying a battered Stetson that had once been black, and now was dust-covered and faded by the sun until it was a sort of vague, dirty gray.

"You know whose this is?"

Grant knelt beside her, holding the hat out. She knew, and something died in her, the ghost of the faith that had clung to her through the hours since Rick had left the Bent R.

"Rick's," she said. "He couldn't have done it, Grant."

"This'll be all the proof Graham needs," Jenner said with satisfaction. He poked a finger through the bullet hole in the crown. "You must have come mighty close."

She shuddered and turned her head away, and for a moment she thought she could not go on living, knowing this. Grant would tell Graham about Rick's quarrel with Lou the afternoon before. Wildew had heard it. He'd tell, too. And if they put her on the stand, she would have to say the same thing.

"I'll hitch up the wagon," Grant was saying. "We'll take the body into town. We'll tell Graham. It'll be up to him."

Very gently she laid Lou's head down and rose. She faced Jenner, trembling, her hands knotted at her sides. "Grant, they'll hang Rick."

He took her hands, looking down at her, the red sunlight on his face. "You still love him, don't you?"

"No. I don't love him at all. I'm sure of that now, but I wouldn't want to see him hang. Maybe somebody left the hat here to frame him."

"We've got to tell Graham," Jenner said doggedly.

For the first time in her life she felt there was real strength in Grant Jenner, strength and courage, and she had a haunting feeling that he would go after Rick himself and be killed.

"All right, we'll tell Graham, but promise me you'll leave this to the sheriff. For me, Grant. I don't want Rick's blood on your hands."

"Or my blood on his hands. Which is it?"

"I don't want to lose you," she said tonelessly. "Will you promise?"

"I promise," he said, and turned toward the barn.

She walked into the house, trying to understand this,

and failing. Other people wanted Lou dead. Rick was not a man who would have killed Lou this way. A few minutes later she rode away from the Bent R, sitting on the spring seat of the wagon beside Jenner, Lou's body behind them in the bed covered by a canvas. Rick's hat was back there, too. *It must have been him,* she thought. *If it was, they ought to hang him.*

# CHAPTER 15

## Buckshot

WILDEW MUST HAVE STOOD THERE STARING AT RICK for a full minute, his pale blue eyes expressionless. There was no trace of regret on his tough, narrow face. He said, "You're gonna have quite a wait, kid." He laid Rick's gun on the table and sat down on the floor near the door, his back to the wall. He rolled a smoke, asking, "Want a cigarette?"

Rick wanted one, but his pride would not let him ask Wildew for it. He said, "No."

Wildew finished his smoke and then dropped flat on his back, lying in front of the door so that it could not be opened without disturbing him. He said, "You passed up a good deal, kid. Ten thousand from Kinnear to help wind up his dirty business. Fleming takes five hundred and thinks he's got a bargain." Wildew chuckled. "Just as happy as a kid with a gum drop. Well, I'll have the stake I want and I won't be splitting it with you."

"You don't figure anybody'll be fool enough to think I plugged Lou, do you?" Rick demanded.

"That's exactly what I figure. Kinnear'll make a circus out of your trial. It's just what he wants. He'll

158

have reporters here from Portland. They'll write you up big, gunman that turns on his boss because he wouldn't let you marry his granddaughter. When Kinnear gets done with you, he'll be the best known man in the state."

Rick stared at Wildew, lying there as motionless as a log, hands under his head, eyes closed. Rick was not fooled. Wildew might drop off to sleep, or just lie there, perfectly relaxed. He had a talent for resting anywhere under any circumstances, but the slightest sound would bring him back to a keen sense of awareness.

Silently Rick strained at the ropes that bound him. No use. Fleming had done his job well. There was no slack, no slipping of the knots. Escape was impossible even if Wildew was not in the room with him. They would not kill him outright, not if Kinnear wanted to make something big out of his trial. He'd put on a circus all right, and he'd get the publicity he wanted. He might be elected to Congress, but he would never marry Lola Spargo.

Kinnear could dictate the politics of the county; he could control the sheriff's office and the bank, and he could intimidate a jury so that Rick Malone would be convicted of murder. But no matter how big and powerful Kinnear became, Lola was one person who would not be humbled by him. Rick's mind fastened upon that thought, and he found some satisfaction in it.

The hours dragged by. It was useless to appeal to Wildew. Even if there was a chance of persuading the gunman to release him, Rick could not bring himself to try. Now, looking ahead, Rick's mind leaped from one future event to another that seemed destined. Rawlins would be murdered. Rick would be released at the precise moment that would make his capture by Graham

159

a simple matter. They would take him to jail. A sense of futility settled upon him. He was powerless to prevent any of these things.

Rick mentally tabulated the few people who might help him. He thought first of Lola who would do all she could for him, but it would not be enough. Curly Hale? Probably he would not turn a hand. He had been suspicious of Rick when he had left Hatchet, and when he returned, he would be so busy trying to save Hatchet he would have no time for anything else.

Nan? Rick could not be sure, but he thought she would hate him. She would probably believe that he had killed Rawlins exactly as Kinnear and Wildew wanted her to. Jenner? It would be the same with him. Jenner did not like him, and the suspicion that Nan had loved Rick would add to his dislike. Tebo? No chance at all if he was tied in with Kinnear and Cord Graham as he undoubtedly was.

That was the list. Lola was the only one he could depend on. To make it worse, Rick had no money to hire a good lawyer. It probably made little difference with Kinnear controlling the court. The cards were stacked. He stared at Wildew, a violent burst of fury flaming in him. He shouted, "Matt."

Wildew sat up and rubbed his eyes. He rose and lifted a corner of the blanket that covered a window. It was daylight. He jerked the blanket down and blew out the lamp. He turned to Rick, his cool, meaningless smile on his lips.

"What's biting you, kid?" Wildew asked.

"I've been thinking," Rick said. "Had a lot of time. It's funny, just damned funny, you saving my life and taking me along with you, and now you're putting a rope on my neck."

"What's funny about that?"

"It's always funny when anybody's as dead wrong as I've been, ain't it? I used to think you were the biggest man on earth. I even gave you credit for having some principles."

"Oh hell, are you harping on that again? I'll tell you something, kid. I've always had one principle. Just one. I figure to do what's best for Matt Wildew. If you'd thought as much of Rick Malone, you wouldn't be sitting there, tied up like a calf for branding."

"You're making one mistake, Matt. Lola knows how I happened to leave Hatchet. She knows the time. It won't jibe. You told us Lou was already dead."

Wildew shrugged. "It'd be just her word and yours. You won't get nowhere with that yarn, not with Kinnear handling the trial."

"Another thing," Rick said. "You claim the soft spot I've got will keep me from drilling you. It won't. When I get my hands on a gun, I'll smoke you down and I'll laugh in your face while I'm doing it."

"You'll try maybe," Wildew said, "if you get a chance which you won't. If you think you're gonna get me to cut you loose just so we can find out who's the fastest, you're loco. I'm satisfied to let 'em string you up."

"You're scared," Rick taunted. "You know damned well I can beat you to the draw."

"I was never scared of anything in my life," Wildew said. "I ain't slowed up yet. I will in time. That's why I kept you around and taught you all I know about gunfighting. I figured you had sense enough to stick with me. You were my insurance against the day when I would slow up, but you had to start thinking too much." He shrugged. "I'm just taking care of my own future."

161

Wildew said it casually enough, but Rick sensed that the gunman felt as strongly about this as he was capable of feeling about anything. It explained why Wildew had stooped to a game he would ordinarily have had no part in. His worry about his future had been greater than Rick had thought.

"You're a miserable, crawling thing," Rick said bitterly. "You always claimed you weren't like Fleming, but hell, you're worse. You belong under a rock right beside him."

"Go ahead," Wildew said indifferently. "Talk as ornery as you want to if it makes you feel good."

A horse was coming down the road. Wildew wheeled toward the door and opened it a crack, right hand on gun butt. The rider drew up and Wildew threw the door open and stepped out. Rick heard Fleming say, "I done it, and the girl took a few shots at me like you figured she would. Dug a hunk of meat out of my leg, too, damn her."

"Bad?"

"Naw. I'm all right."

"I'll get to town and tell Kinnear. I'll put your horse in the shed. Don't leave Malone."

"You're damned right I won't," Fleming said wickedly.

He came into the house, bloodshot eyes pinned on Rick. Wildew followed, giving him a studying look. "I don't give a damn about Malone," Wildew said, "but if you beat him up, the sheriff is gonna wonder about it and it'll make Malone's story sound good. Don't touch him. Savvy?"

"Graham won't believe nothing Malone says," Fleming muttered. "He'll do anything Kinnear says."

"You're a fool," Wildew said. "Even Kinnear has to

162

make things look right. You touch Malone and you won't get your five hundred. And I'll tell you something else. I'll burn you down myself if I have to chase you to hell-enback."

"You're talking mighty tough," Fleming said defiantly.

"Got any doubts about me being tough?" Wildew asked.

"All right, all right," Fleming said.

"Keep him inside until the posse shows up, then let him walk out of here. Kinnear wants him taken alive. Remember that, too."

"He'll make a run for it."

"He won't get far without a horse, and if he don't get his hands on a gun, he won't make no trouble. You get your pay when Graham locks him up and not before. And don't let the posse see you. Savvy?"

"Sure, sure," Fleming said irritably. "Get moving."

Wildew wheeled and walked out. Fleming closed the door and stood at a window watching until Wildew rode away. Then he swung around and came to Rick's chair, his eyes filled with a deep and passionate hatred.

"It ain't worth five hundred dollars to let you walk out of here alive," Fleming said. "Not after you tried to drown me in a horse trough and plugged Deke. He was my friend, the only friend I ever had."

"Getting plugged in the back is better than swinging from a rope," Rick said. "When you let me out of here, why don't you burn me down?"

Fleming glowered at him, and then limped back to the window. With the light stronger in the room now Rick could see the dark splotch on his pants leg.

"So Nan tagged you," Rick said. "You go to the doc and he'll ask you some questions. What are you going

163

to tell him?"

"I won't go to no doc."

"Then you'll get blood poison. Build up a fire and I'll heat an iron. I'll take care of it for you."

"That'd be real smart, now wouldn't it?" Fleming jeered.

"Blood poison's a hell of a way to die," Rick said. "Hurts something fierce. I remember a man in Santa Fe who got gangrene. It was several years ago, but I'll never forget how he howled. Couldn't stand the pain."

"Shut up," Fleming shouted. "Damn it, shut up your tater trap."

Rick let it go at that. He had planted the seed. If there was time, it would grow. Fleming remained by the window, and again time dragged out for him. Presently a wagon creaked by; he saw Fleming stiffen and draw back from the window.

"Who is it?" Rick asked.

"Jenner and the Rawlins girl. You let out a holler and I'll let 'em have you. Jenner would like to put a window in your skull, I reckon."

The clatter of the wagon died and again there was no sound but Fleming's heavy breathing and the squeal of floor boards as he moved restlessly around the room. His leg was hurting him, Rick thought, and there was a good chance he would break under the weight of his worry about his wound.

"You oughtta get that leg taken care of," Rick said softly. "I'd hate to see a dog die that way."

Fleming wheeled, panicky now, and Rick saw he had overdone it. Fleming raised a hand and struck him across the side of the head, a savage blow that rocked him. "Open your mug again and I'll forget what Wildew said. I'll fix your purty face so even the Spargo woman won't know. . ."

The door slammed open. Fleming had his back to it. He wheeled, grabbing his gun and lifting it from leather.

Lola stood there, a shotgun in her hands. She screamed, "Don't try it. I'll kill you if you do."

But Fleming, out of his head from worry about his wound and knowing he could expect no mercy from Rick, made his try. His gun came on up, hammer back, and then Lola let go. The room echoed with the report; the charge of buckshot caught Fleming in his middle and tore a great hole in him. He went back and down, gun falling from his hand, and he was dead before he hit the floor.

Lola ran into the room, not looking at the body. "You all right, Rick?"

"I am if I can get I out of here. There's a knife in my pocket."

She found the knife and opened it; she cut the rope, fumbling a little, unable to control her trembling. When the rope fell away, Rick rose and walked swiftly to the table. He gripped it, dizzy now that he was on his feet.

"Go outside," Rick said.

Lola turned and fled from the house. Rick knew she was sick. The sight of a dead man was always ugly, but a man killed by buckshot at this distance was enough to make anyone sick. Even Rick, familiar with death, could not bring himself to look at the bloody shape on the floor. He put his gun into leather, still dizzy; he held himself there until his head quit whirling, then he went outside, closing the door behind him.

Lola was leaning against the wall. She had dropped her shotgun, and when Rick reached her, he thought she was going to faint. He asked, "Can you walk?"

"I . . . I think so."

"Let's get into the shed. We don't want to be here if somebody comes along."

He put an arm around her. She was still trembling, the corners of her mouth working with a crazy, spasmodic twitching. They reached the shed, and Rick saw that his horse was still there. Lola sat down in the barn litter, her head bowed.

Rick walked around, rubbing his wrists and getting the circulation back into his legs. For several minutes he said nothing, knowing that only time would restore Lola's self-control. Presently he came to her and sat down beside her.

"I was a dead man till you showed up," he said. "Even if Fleming hadn't plugged me which he was hankering to do, the posse would have nailed me for Rawlins' murder and Kinnear would have strung me up."

She looked at him, her face pale. The twitching was gone now. "I killed him," she breathed. "I killed him."

"He'd have killed you if you hadn't. Chances are he'd have drilled me, too. Nobody's gonna worry about that ornery son kicking the bucket but Wildew and Kinnear." He put an arm around her and held her shoulders against his chest. "For hours I sat there with nothing to do but think, and all the time I knew you were the only one I could count on. I didn't figure you'd save my hide, though. Not the way you did."

"I wouldn't have shot him if he hadn't pulled his gun," she said miserably.

"You couldn't do nothing else," he said. "You've got to think of it that way."

For several minutes he held her, hard pressed by the knowledge that they should be riding, but knowing she wasn't able.

166

"How'd you happen to find me?" he asked.

"I was worried about you," she said. "After I thought about it, it didn't seem right, Nan sending Wildew after you that way, so I saddled up, thinking I'd ride to the Bent R. I had to find out what had happened. I stayed off the road after the sun came up until I saw Jenner and Nan coming. I stopped them. They had Rawlins' body in the wagon."

"They think I killed him?"

"Jenner does," she answered evasively. "Nan saw the man who did the killing, but she couldn't identify him. She shot at him, and when Jenner found your hat, there was a bullet hole in it."

"Fleming done the job. He must have put the bullet hole in the hat himself." He rose. "We've got to ride. I don't know what to do, but we've got to get out of here."

"I left my horse by the river," she said. "I thought they'd have you somewhere close to the Bent R. I didn't really expect to find you, but I thought I'd look in these old houses. Then when I saw your horse in the shed here, I knew."

He saddled up and backed his horse out of the stall. Fleming was the one man who could have cleared him, for he was the kind who would have broken under pressure, and Rick doubted that either Wildew or Kinnear would. But there was no sense in telling Lola.

"Can you ride now?" he asked.

She nodded. "They'll search Hatchet for you. I'd take you there if I thought I could hide you."

"You head for home. I'll make out."

She tilted her head back, her chin thrust defiantly at him. "What do you take me for, Rick? You wouldn't be in this jam if it wasn't for me."

"That don't make no never mind. Only thing I'm sure of is I ain't gonna run and I won't keep hiding."

He wanted to tell her that he had too much to live for now to throw it away by running, that he had to keep her respect, and a man hiding and running could not do that. But this was not the time. He would tell her later when he was cleared. Even as that thought crossed his mind, there was the balancing thought that he could not think of anything that could clear him.

"You've got to hide for a while," she said. "Something will happen, Rick, but you've got to stay out of jail. If they get you, you'll never prove you didn't kill Rawlins."

"I won't hide," he said stubbornly. "Not forever."

"Oh, Rick, I don't mean forever. Just until we can think of what to do."

He rubbed his stubble-covered face, finding it hard to think. He had to go after Wildew and Kinnear, but if he faced Wildew now, tired and hungry and with stiff wrists, Wildew would kill him.

"Where'll I hide?" he asked finally.

"Can we get into town without being seen?"

"It's daylight. People have eyes."

"We'll stay along the river. The willows are thick. I think we can do it."

"What have you got in your head?"

"We need time," she said. "Kinnear doesn't have any real friends in the valley and you have more than you think. We've just got to let it simmer until something happens."

That was like a woman, he thought, hoping for something to happen, but she was right in one way. He needed time. He asked, "You're trying to talk me into hiding in town. That it?"

She nodded. "In Mary Dolan's house. I know her. I think she'll do it."

Crazy. Completely crazy, but it might work for a few hours. He wasn't sure Mary Dolan would hide him, but he was sure of one thing. It was the last place Graham and Kinnear would look for him.

"All right," he said. "We'll try it."

# CHAPTER 16

## Blackmail

LOLA DID NOT FEEL THE CONFIDENCE SHE WANTED Rick to believe she had. She could not think of a plan that would clear him, and she was not certain Mary Dolan would give him a refuge. Even if she did agree to hide him, his chance of getting into town and into Mary's house without being seen was a slim one.

The smartest thing Rick could do was to get out of the country while he could, but she knew he wouldn't do that and she realized with a sense of guilt that she didn't want him to. She would never see him again if he did. That was the one thing she couldn't stand.

They kept close to the river, the double row of willows between them and the road. If anyone saw them, it was not likely they would be recognized, and it was not probable they would have trouble if they did. There had not yet been time for the news of Rawlins' murder to spread through the valley. The posse was the one real danger, but Graham would expect to find Rick near the Dolan house.

The feeling of guilt about killing Fleming was gone. from her now. As Rick had said, she'd been given no choice. Her worry now was Rick's safety. If she hadn't talked to him in town, he would not have been caught in Kinnear's trap. But regardless of that, she would still have been compelled to help him.

She loved him. Foolish, she thought, for when this was over he would probably ride out of the valley. She had known him such a short time. She wasn't even sure that his feeling for Nan had changed. But none of it made any difference. She loved him.

She glanced at Rick often, riding in the slack way of a man who has been ground down by weariness until his reactions were slower than usual. His face showed a dark smudge of stubble; his eyes were red-veined from lack of sleep. She wanted to reach out and touch him, to let him know how she felt. She couldn't. She could not burden him with a feeling of obligation. She had done enough to him already.

They were not far from town when they heard the beat of hoofs on the other side of the river. They reined up, glimpsing Graham and his posse going by on the road.

Neither Kinnear nor Wildew was with them.

The posse would be gone for hours, Lola thought. She wondered what they would do when they found Fleming's body in the Dolan house and that Rick was nowhere around. Probably they would search the other houses and it would be evening at least before they came back to town.

When the posse had gone by, Rick gave her a wry grin. "They'll have a ride," he said.

They went on, and out of the countless plans and hazy ideas that crowded Lola's mind, one began taking definite shape. The river, slow-moving and shallow at this point, made a wide curve around the edge of town.

170

They rode through the willows and fording the stream, pulled up in the gravel on the town side. Mary's house was less than a block away.

"Stay here till I see Mary," Lola said. "It won't take long."

He hesitated, then said grudgingly, "All right, I'll wait."

She had no way of knowing what he had in mind, but judging from the grim set of his lean face, she had a feeling that he had decided upon some plan of his own. She put her horse through the willows and rode on across the empty lot and the alley, and dismounted at Mary's back porch. She knocked, and she was not surprised when she saw the bitter and unforgiving expression on Mary's face when she opened the door.

"I want to talk to you," Lola said. "I'm here to do a favor and ask for one."

"When I swap favors with you," Mary snapped, "I'll be a whole lot crazier'n I am now."

"Not even for Rick Malone?"

Mary hesitated, then she said, "Come in," and stepped aside.

Lola went into the kitchen and sat down on a straight-backed chair. Mary closed the door and moved to the stove. She put her hands on her wide hips, the expression of hostility still on her face. The kitchen was fragrant with the smell of baking pies. Mary must have been working in the kitchen for some time. Sweat made a faint shine across her forehead. It struck Lola that Mary had no real troubles. Perhaps she was happier than the others who were caught in the web of Kinnear's scheming. Her injuries were behind her.

"What's this about Rick?" Mary asked.

"I want to say one thing before I tell you about Rick,"

Lola said. "I know how you felt about Vance and I don't blame you, but I hope you won't feel the same way about me."

"You're his sister," Mary said truculently.

"Did it ever occur to you that Joe Kinnear might be more to blame for what happened to Hank than Vance was?"

"I don't like Kinnear, either."

"I'm going to fight to keep Tebo from getting Hatchet," Lola said. "Indirectly that means Kinnear. If I win, I'll give your place back to you."

"Surprising," Mary said skeptically. "Downright surprising, coming from you."

"You don't know me very well," Lola said. "I guess nobody does, but I want to live here. Maybe in time people will accept me for what I am and forget the things they've said about me and that Vance was my brother."

"You must figure on living a million years," Mary said. "What about Rick?"

"I said I came to exchange one favor for another. I've told you mine. The favor I want is about Rick. Lou Rawlins was murdered early this morning. Kinnear framed Rick for it. A posse has left town to bring him."

Shocked, Mary pulled up a chair and sat down. "He wouldn't have killed that old goat. He couldn't marry Nan if he did." Her lips tightened. "Maybe you didn't know about that."

"I knew. You're right when you said he couldn't have done it. Wildew held him prisoner in your old place while Fleming shot Rawlins. Then Fleming came back and was guarding Rick while Wildew came to town. They planned to turn Rick loose so Graham could take him. That's Rick's story and I believe it."

172

Mary jerked a handkerchief from her pocket and wiped her face. She said, "This is coming a little too fast for me."

"I don't know how to clear Rick," Lola went on, "but, I have an idea I want to try. I'm asking you to hide him for a few hours. He was tied up in a chair for most of the night and some of this morning. He needs sleep and something to eat. Will you take care of him?"

"What's Rick to you?"

Lola rose, her face coloring. "Let's say I'm nothing to him. Will you do it?"

"I'm still behind in your story. How did Rick get away from Fleming?"

"I killed Fleming. Rick came into town with me."

Mary snorted. "You expect me to believe that?"

"You don't have to believe anything. I just want you to take care of Rick for a few hours."

"Sure I'll do that, but it'd be for him and not on account of your fine intentions about giving my place back. Fetch him in."

"It may get you into trouble."

"With who?"

"Kinnear and Graham."

"That suits me fine. I can't think of anybody I'd rather get into trouble with than that pair. Go on, fetch Rick in." As Lola walked to the door, Mary added, "And maybe I can get some sense out of your yarn if I talk to Rick. Why would Wildew hold him prisoner, for instance?"

"He sold out to Kinnear."

Lola left then, not wanting the rest of it to come out. Mary might change her mind if she knew that Rick had broken with Nan and had left the Bent R to work for her. She rode back to the river, feeling a keen sense of

173

relief when she saw that Rick was still there.

"It's all right," Lola said. "Walk in. I'll leave your horse in the stable."

He scratched his cheek, looking thoughtfully at her. "If I get Mary into trouble . . ."

"You won't. Not with Graham out of town. After dark you can come out to Hatchet. I have a hunch Graham will look for you there on his way back to town, but he won't think of looking there again."

Rick's jaw set stubbornly. "Lola, let's get one thing straight. There's only one way to settle this. I've got to go after Wildew and Kinnear. This is more'n just me. It's you and Nan and everybody else in the valley."

"Right now it's you, Rick."

He shook his head. "It's like you said about Vance. You can't go back and live his life over for him. All you can do is to try to right some of the things he did. Same with me. I can't live the last six years over, but I aim to make the rest of my life different. While I'm doing something about Kinnear, maybe I can clear myself."

"Not if you're in jail."

"Yeah, that's right, but I ain't going to your place to hide."

"All right, Rick. Just go to Mary's."

"Where are you going?"

"To the hotel. I didn't rest much last night, either."

"I know," he said, and stepping down, handed her the reins. "I want to see Graham when he gets back. You fetch him over, or let me know as soon as he gets into town."

"I'll let you know," she said, and watched him walk through the willows and cross the empty lot.

She waited until he disappeared into Mary's house, then she rode back across the river and came into town from the north, leading Rick's horse. She stopped at the stable, saying, "I found this animal between here and Hatchet. You know who he belongs to?"

The stableman's mouth sagged open. "Malone! That's who he belongs to. He stole another horse or he's afoot!"

"What makes you say that?"

"Don't you know?" When Lola shook her head, he said, "That ornery son plugged old man Rawlins this morning and the sheriff's on his trail now."

Lola shrugged. She said indifferently, "Well, take care of his horse," and left the stable.

She went directly to the bank. She knew that Tebo closed at noon, but it was not quite twelve, and she saw with relief that the bank was open. She waited until Tebo finished with a customer, then she opened the gate at the end of the counter and waited until Tebo came to her.

"I didn't expect to see you today," Tebo said. "Did Hale leave for the railroad?"

She nodded. "But that isn't what I came in for. You've heard about Rawlins."

He nodded, his face grim. "I can't believe Malone did it. It's not his kind of killing, and I don't see no reason he could have had for doing it."

"Don't you know what happened?"

Tebo shook his head. "Do you?"

"I know all of it," she said, "and I expect you to do something about it. Kinnear framed him."

"Could be that way," Tebo admitted. "Joe would like to see Rawlins out of the way, and he'd want to get square with Malone for that licking he took." He frowned. "How do you know so much about it?"

"Never mind about that," she said sharply. "I'm worried about Rick. If we don't do something, Graham

175

will put him in jail and if it comes to a trial, Kinnear will convict him. Isn't that right?"

"Reckon it is," Tebo said, puzzled. "He's never lost a case he really wanted to win since he got elected district attorney, but I don't savvy why you're concerned about him."

"We'll just call that my business. I said you had to help Rick. You know Joe's crooked. You know what he's made you do, and you told me yesterday he owned Graham. Now Wildew has hired out to him. If we're ever going to lick him, we've got to do it before they get their hands on Rick."

"I can't touch it," Tebo said flatly.

"Then I'll blackmail you," Lola said. "You get Rick out of this, or I'll break the promise I made yesterday. Rick will go after Wildew, and I know Kinnear too well to think he'll take a chance and let it be a fair fight."

"What can I do?" Tebo cried. "This isn't my kind of business."

"You'll make it your kind. You did talk too much yesterday. If you don't help Rick, I'll tell everybody in town why you're doing Kinnear's dirty work."

"Nobody will believe you," Tebo shouted, white-faced. "You can't make me do a thing."

"Your wife will believe me," Lola said. "She's the first one I'll go to."

Tebo gripped the counter, shoulders sagging, a beaten, harried man. He asked, "All right. Tell me what you want me to do."

"I don't know. It's your problem. I suppose Graham will be back sometime this evening. I'll give you until then."

Turning, she walked out, leaving him standing there and staring at her back.

# CHAPTER 17

## Shadow of a Noose

IT WAS LATE AFTERNOON WHEN RICK WOKE. FOR A moment he could not remember where he was. He had slept like a dead man, and it took time for the opiate of sleep to wear off. The sun was beating at him through the west window. He got up, yawning, and then he heard the low hum of talk from the kitchen. He recognized Jenner's voice, then Nan's, and finally Mary Dolan's, and the full weight of his trouble fell upon him.

He began rubbing his wrists. He had wanted time and he had gained enough. His wrists were not as stiff as he had expected. He would be as fast as he ever was; he would kill Wildew or Wildew would kill him. There was no regret in him. Wildew would do anything for the ten thousand Kinnear had promised him; he was a mad dog that must be executed.

Rick took some time with his gun, checking it and making sure that his holster was in exactly the right position. He moved to Mary's mirror and practiced his draw several times, remembering how often he had seen Wildew do this very thing when he faced a gunfight.

"Don't practice too much just before you tackle a man." Wildew would say. "Takes the edges off. Just be sure you're in shape. That adds up to a lot of things, kid. The gun and the holster and your eyes and wrist and arm. If you ain't pulling right, figure out some way to put the fight off, or they'll be throwing clods in your face."

Rick was right. He felt it. He thought about Wildew

177

saying he had kept Rick around as insurance against the day when he would be too old to earn a gunhand's pay. It explained a great many things. Now they would face each other. Perhaps it had been destined from the first.

Wildew had made another thing clear, too. Rick had given him credit for the principles he had talked about, but they had not been principles at all. Everything he had ever done or said had been designed for two purposes, to keep him alive and earn more money. It was strictly a matter of money that had sent him to Kinnear, that had brought about the murder of Lou Rawlins and had pinned the murder on Rick.

With both Fleming and Wildew dead, Kinnear might break. Early in the day Rick had thought that with Fleming gone, there was no chance to clear himself. It might be only wishful thinking, but he had some hope that Kinnear would break if enough pressure was put on him. Rick could put that pressure on Kinnear if Wildew was out of the way. He had told Lola to bring Graham to him or let him know when the sheriff got back to town. Now, thinking about it clearly, it seemed a wild hope. Graham would not listen as long as Kinnear was alive. This was better.

Rick opened the door and stepped into the kitchen. Nan saw him and cried out, a hand coming up to her mouth. Jenner sat motionless as if paralyzed, eyes on Rick in the way of a man who was seeing something he could not believe.

Mary laughed. "Surprise, isn't it? Well sir, he got me to take him in under false pretenses. I didn't know you two had busted up, Nan." She nodded at Rick. "I've heard the whole story now, and all I've got to say is that Nan made a poor choice."

"Don't say that," Nan whispered. "What are you

doing here, Rick?"

"Sleeping. I was hungry and Mary fed me. It's all written down in the book. She gets an extra star in her crown when she goes to heaven."

"I'm too wicked to go to heaven," Mary said lightly.

Jenner, white-faced, had turned his body so that his right hand was hidden from Rick. Now it moved covertly toward his gun, eyes fixed on Rick. Mary saw what he planned to do. She scooted down in her chair and brought a foot up in a slashing kick that caught Jenner's wrist the instant his hand closed over gun butt. He yelped and jerked his hand away.

"See what I mean, Nan?" Mary asked. "If he had the guts a man ought to have, he'd stand up and pull. Instead he tried to sneak in a shot. If my judgment of our friend Rick is right, he wouldn't do a sneaking trick like that."

"He's a killer," Jenner said hotly. "I wouldn't have no chance with him on an even draw. I was just trying to get my gun on him so I could take him in. If he pulled, he'd plug me."

"No," Rick said. "I like Nan too well. You're going to marry him, ain't you, Nan?"

Nan rose and came to stand beside Jenner, her hand on his shoulder. She said defiantly, "That's right, Rick. I didn't know how I felt about Grant until this morning."

"I had a hunch yesterday when we left the Diamond J," Rick said. "You were feeling sorry for him. When a woman feels that way, she thinks more of a man than she lets on."

"You're a pair of locoed kids," Mary snapped. "So much has happened that you've got kinks in your ropes."

"There's no kink in my rope," Rick said. "Reckon I

should have told you how it was with me and Nan, but I had to have some time. If I'd gone after Wildew this morning, he'd have plugged me sure. Now I can take him."

Mary rose and started toward him, then stopped as if a new thought had struck her. "It's Lola, isn't it, Rick?"

"Yes." Rick looked at Nan, and he saw her as a girl, pretty and desirable, her blonde hair freshly curled, her dark blue eyes meeting his, but still a girl with the changeable mind of one who lacks maturity. "I guess we were a pair of locoed kids, all right. I'd never been around anyone like you, and Lou had kept you under a tight rein, so it was natural we'd cotton to each other. Now I can see it's a good thing it worked out this way."

"A damned good thing," Jenner said vehemently, "but we ain't settling nothing. I aim to take you to the jug and you're gonna stay there till Graham gets back to town."

"Don't make trouble for yourself," Rick said. "Not if you want to live long enough to marry Nan. It's Wildew I want and then Kinnear. If you had the sense of a loon, you'd know you won't have peace on this range till Kinnear's dead." He nodded at Nan. "I didn't kill Lou. I'd like for you to believe that."

"I . . . I wish I could," she whispered, "but I don't know."

"You think I did, Jenner?"

"It ain't your kind of killing," Jenner admitted grudgingly, "but how do you figure on changing Graham's mind about it?"

"I'm hoping to get the truth out of Kinnear. If I can't, it'll be up to Nan. She's the only one who saw the man who done it."

Rick walked to the stove, picked up a cup and filled it

180

with coffee. He drank it, eyes on Nan. The silence ran on for a full minute. Mary, too, was watching Nan. Jenner got to his feet, kicking his chair back in a sudden burst of temper.

"What do you expect Nan to say?" Jenner demanded. "It wasn't really light and she was worked up, shooting at him and knowing Lou was lying out there. Hell, she can't swear to nothing."

"Fleming is a bigger man than I am." Rick said. "He had his hat on his head. I didn't have mine."

"Think, Nan," Mary urged. "You must have had some impression about him even if you couldn't see him well."

"Damn it," Jenner, bellowed. "Let her alone. She's had enough trouble for one day without worrying her with this."

"If I live," Rick said, "I'm going to marry Lola if she'll have me. I want to live here. I've got to have my name cleared if I'm going to do that."

"I can't think, Rick," Nan whispered. "I just can't think. He was quite a ways off and he was running. I don't know whether he had a hat on or not."

"Wouldn't prove nothing anyhow," Jenner muttered.

Rick put his cup down. "I reckon Jenner will make you a good husband, Nan. Long as Lou was alive he'd knuckled down so long it got to be a habit. Now it'll be different. Same thing with this county. With Kinnear gone, we'll have honest law and maybe Tebo will run the bank different. We need that, too."

"You've always been a drifter," Jenner flung at him. "You've been a gunslinger. You'll never settle down. It ain't in you to change."

"I've already changed," Rick said quietly. "I can thank Nan for that. I followed along behind Matt

181

because it was a habit, but the older I got, the more I wasn't satisfied doing it. So I busted with him. You know why, Nan, and you know I couldn't have drygulched Lou."

Still she said nothing, and he knew that if she ever did, she would be lying for him because she felt she owed him that much. She simply didn't know. Even if she did clear him, Jenner would never be sure and he'd talk. Then other people would wonder and they would never forget. Their suspicion would follow him as long as he lived in the valley.

Rick turned to Jenner. "You know where Wildew is?"

"In the Stag," Jenner answered. "Or he was a little while ago."

Rick glanced at his watch. It was not yet six. He said, "Go tell Wildew that he's gonna tell the truth about Lou's killing or I'm coming after him. Tell him to be in front of the Stag at six."

"You can't do it," Mary cried. "You won't be able to forget he was your friend."

"No," Rick said. "He never was my friend, or he wouldn't have fixed it so I'd hang. I've got to do it this way." He nodded at Jenner. "Get moving. Tell him."

Jenner picked up his hat and walked out of the house. For a moment Rick stood there, looking at Nan who was crying now, and he thought of how it might have been. He remembered the first time he had kissed her; he remembered how often she had wanted him to tell Lou how it was with them and he had kept putting it off. Then when he had finally forced the issue, she would not go with him. He thought, *Things work out. It would have been wrong if she had gone with me.*

He turned to Mary. "Everybody's been wrong about Lola. She's been dragged through a lot of misery, but

182

she's still the finest woman I know. Tell her I love her if I don't get a chance to tell her."

Tight-lipped, Mary said, "I'll tell her."

Rick left the house, bare-headed. He looked at the sun, hanging low in a clear sky above the western rim of the valley, and he walked around the block so that he would come into Main Street from the west. It was one of the things Wildew had taught him. He had often said, "Make the other fellow face the sun. If it's a tight squeeze, that little margin makes the difference."

He glanced at his watch again. Almost six. He came into Main Street, the sun to his back, the red light very sharp upon the false fronts, the street dirt that had been mud yesterday was now hardened by the day's dry heat. He made one final check of his gun and left it riding loosely in leather.

He looked at the horse trough where he almost drowned Fleming; he looked at the spot where Cardigan had fallen. Then something struck him he had not thought about before. His eyes lifted to the windows above the bank. Joe Kinnear's office was up there. He'd be watching him. Rick was officially wanted for murder. If Kinnear cut him down, the law would not touch him. Not Chinook County law.

Then the batwings of the Stag were flung open and Wildew stepped out of the saloon. With a sudden rush of panic Rick thought, *Why didn't I figure out where Kinnear would be?* Now that it was too late, he wished he had seen Lola once more.

183

# CHAPTER 18

## At Sundown

THE NEWS MUST HAVE REACHED BALD ROCK THAT Rick Malone had not been found, that Fleming's body had been discovered, blown half in two by a charge of buckshot. Or at least Kinnear and Wildew knew that something was wrong or the posse would have been back long ago. Wildew and Kinnear would not be surprised, then, that Rick had turned up in town and that he was gunning for them.

Rick considered this as Wildew came into the street, and it added to his conviction that Kinnear was the more dangerous of the two. Then the moment of panic passed. Again one of Wildew's teachings beat against Rick's mind. "Don't divide your attention. If you've got more'n one man to handle, don't start fretting about the second one till the first one's out of the way."

Rick raised his eyes to Kinnear's office window, mentally measuring the distance and judging where he would be when the lawyer started firing. There was a horse trough to Rick's right. If he could reach it, he would be out of Kinnear's sight.

Wildew was moving toward Rick, the familiar, cool smile on his lips, his lean, sharp-featured face impassive. If he had considered the possibility of death, he gave no sign of it. Rick stood motionless, waiting, his shadow long before him, right hand within inches of gun butt.

"You ain't man enough to do this job, kid," Wildew called. "I'm the teacher. You're just the pupil.

Remember?"

Rick said nothing. For these few seconds Kinnear was out of his mind, but another thought jarred him. This was an old scene, an old game, vicious and brutal, a game in which a man must use every trick he had to save his life just as Rick had taken the position that placed the sun to his back. But this would be the last time.

Wildew was the symbol of all that was behind him. When he went down before Rick's gun, the past would be cut like a sharp knife slashing a taut ribbon with one quick stroke. Lola stood for what lay ahead; Wildew stood for the past that was gone.

"You've got a soft spot, kid," Wildew called. He was coming on, slower now, frowning a little as if expecting Rick to break and make his play, but Rick stood as immobile as a figure of granite. "I told you I'd kill you. When you go for your cutter, you'll be throwing down on a man who taught you everything you know. You ain't good enough, kid. You just ain't good enough."

It was one of Wildew's favorite tricks. "Gunfights are won in a man's head," Wildew used to say. He always talked when he moved against an enemy, talked and worried him and slowed his draw, but Rick knew the trick and it didn't work.

Wildew was close now, close enough to make his play, close enough for Rick to see the pale blue color of his eyes, the hard, cruel line of his mouth. Then the thing happened that Rick had been expecting, but not in the way he had expected. Two shots sounded from Kinnear's office, one hard upon the other.

Rick felt no bullets; he did not hear the snap of a slug passing close to his head. There was no lift of the street dirt that might have been kicked up by a stray bullet. He

185

would have been aware of some of these things if Kinnear had fired at him. Then it struck him that Kinnear had not shot at him; he had been knocked out of the fight. Someone else had taken chips in the game.

Wildew must have had the same thought. Now he drew, and in that one short breath of time Rick's hand closed over the hard butt of his gun and he swept his Colt free of leather. There was no thinking in this process; it came from long established habit just as it had when he had fought Deke Cardigan on this same street.

Rick felt the familiar buck of the .44 as the hammer fell, and gunflame danced brightly from the muzzle of his Colt. The roar of the shot rolled out between the false fronts and beat against them and was flung back in a series of dying echoes, and Rick Malone's past died with the going of Matt Wildew. Wildew crumpled, first to his knees as strength went out of them, and he went on down into the dirt of the street.

The slanting sunlight fell upon Rick's back, his long shadow reaching out almost to where Wildew lay. The man's gun was there on the street, unfired, and blood was a spreading stain on his shirt front. Rick came and stood over him as the street was suddenly filled with people. There was no real feeling in him, no regret. It was as if a great weight had been lifted from him, as if destiny had been fulfilled.

There was the beat of hoofs from the east, and Cord Graham's voice rolled in above the thunder of those hoof beats, "Drop your gun, Malone." Then the sound of the driving hoofs stopped, and Graham's voice came again, "You're under arrest for the murder of Lou Rawlins, Malone. Drop your gun."

Rick did not look around; he did not look at the

186

people who stood silently around him and Wildew. His eyes were on the dying man, and he saw that cool, familiar smile on the corners of Wildew's mouth, even now that he was close to death. He knew it. Rick was sure of that, but he did not show the slightest trace of fear of this unknown.

"You're good, kid," Wildew said in a low voice. "Mighty damned good. I taught you better'n I knew I had."

"Tell 'em I didn't plug Rawlins." Rick had never begged anything of Matt Wildew in his life, but he begged now. Graham was out of the saddle, his gun muzzle prodding Rick in the back. "You know what happened, Matt. Tell 'em."

"I don't know a thing about it, kid," Wildew breathed. "Looks like the sheriff wants you. There's just one thing I'm sorry about. I'd like to see you dancing on air and your neck pulled out as long as a washline before I cash in."

"You're dying, Matt," Rick urged. "Tell 'em how you and Kinnear framed me."

"Sorry." Wildew's eyes mocked him. "Kinnear's never lost a case, or so they tell me. You'll hang, kid, you'll hang good and high."

"Get it off your soul," Rick shouted at him. "You've got plenty against you when you face the Almighty. You need one good thing on your side of the ledger."

Wildew lifted a hand as if to push Rick away from him, but the strength was not in him and it fell back beside him, pale eyes glazed with death. He said hoarsely, "Go to hell, kid. You'll be there right behind me."

Then he was gone, eyes staring at the blue sky, blood-streaked lips parted. Rick looked around. Nan and Mary

187

Dolan were there. Grant Jenner. Townsmen he knew casually. He felt the hard pressure of Graham's gun and he was aware that his own was still in his hand.

Nan cried, "He didn't do it, Sheriff. You've got no call to arrest him."

"The hell he didn't," Graham bawled. "Cutting Wildew down won't save his neck."

Tebo was there then, shoving through the crowd, his face pale and haggard. He said, "She's right, Cord. Kinnear framed him. They planted Malone's hat, figuring you'd be stupid enough to believe it was Malone."

Graham passed a hand over his face, shocked by what Tebo had said. He asked, "How come you know so damned much about this?"

"I just shot Kinnear," Tebo said. "He was figuring on cutting Malone down from his window. I got to his office without him knowing it. The door was open. I told him to put his gun up. He turned and shot at me and I got him. Before he died he told me how it was."

Rick wasn't sure whether Tebo was lying; he would never be sure, but it didn't matter. Tebo's word was enough to clear him. He looked at Graham who had moved back, his face taking on the pallor of a man who has lost everything in life that counted to him.

"You plugged Joe?" Graham sucked in a long breath. "You couldn't have done it."

"Go up and take a look," Tebo said wearily. "It was self-defense. You want me?"

"No." Then Graham raised his voice at the crowd. "Get off the street, the lot of you. Tote Wildew over to the Doc's office. Go up and get Kinnear." He wheeled, motioning to the posse. "Put your horses up."

"I want to see you in your office," Tebo said. "You,

too, Malone."

Rick nodded, eyes swinging upward to the second-story windows of the hotel, and he saw Lola's face, pressed against the glass. He shouldered through the crowd to Nan. He said, "Thanks for trying." He looked at Jenner, his face very grim without any trace of the easy smile that usually lingered on his lips. "Take care of her, Jenner, take good care of her."

"I will," Jenner said. "I will."

Rick wheeled away and caught up with Graham and Tebo. They went into the sheriff's office and Graham closed the door. Tebo said, "We know what we've done, Cord, you and me, and I'm not proud of my part in it. Are you?"

Graham lowered his eyes. "Don't know what you're talking about," he muttered.

"Then I'll make it plain. Kinnear owned your soul. You wanted the star just to be big and lord it over everybody else, but you aren't big, Cord. You never were. Just you and me left of the old timers now that Lou's gone. In the old days you weren't anything but a thirty-a-month cowhand nursing Bent R beef. Then Kinnear kicked you upstairs and you took his orders and you shut your eyes when you knew damned well he was the one who plugged Vance."

Graham glared at him, trying to hold his self-respect and his pride and failing. He jerked off his star and threw it on his desk. "All right, Prine. Looks like a new deal all around. I'll be riding."

"Reckon I will, too," Tebo said. "In a few days. It's time for the young ones to run this country. They won't make as big a mess out of it as we have."

"Your bank . . ." Rick began.

"I'll sell out as soon as I can," Tebo said. "I'll sell my

189

house and I'll take my wife and I'll get to hell out of this country. I'm ashamed to stay. I never belonged to Kinnear like Cord did, but I took his orders and I'm ashamed."

Rick held out his hand. "I'm obliged, Tebo. I had you pegged wrong."

Tebo took his hand in a quick, firm grip. "I had you pegged right. You going to marry Lola?"

"If she'll have me."

"She'll have you," Tebo said. "She loves you. She hoorawed me into doing what I did today. You'd have been dead by now if I hadn't."

"Thanks . . ."

"Don't thank me. Go thank Lola."

"I will," Rick said, and wheeled out of the office.

He strode rapidly toward the hotel, knowing that all of his happiness depended on these next few moments. The street still held knots of men talking about what had happened. They looked at him curiously. He went on, ignoring them. There was nothing to say now. Time held all the answers to his problems, time to forget, time to make his place among these people.

He went up the stairs, feeling the clerk's eyes on his back, eyes that held the guarded respect of one who did not want to tangle with him again. The door of Lola's room was open, and when she heard him she turned and waited.

"I'm glad, Rick," she said. "I was afraid for you."

He pulled his gun and threw it onto the bed. He said, "Tebo killed Kinnear and he cleared me. He's gonna sell his bank and leave town. Graham's giving up his star. Tebo said it was Kinnear who killed your brother."

It took a moment for her to gather all of this into her mind and understand what it meant. Then she said, "I wish I knew whether Curly made the deal for our cattle. I'd like to know if we've got a chance to save Hatchet."

He crossed the room to her and took her hands. "I don't think it makes much difference about the cattle. Tebo will fix it for us." He swallowed, searching for words. Everything depended on him saying this right. "I love you. It sounds crazy, us knowing each other for such a little while, but it seems like I've known you for a long time."

"A long time," she murmured. "It has been a long time, Rick, years and years all packed into a few hours. But are you sure you want me?"

"It's the first thing in my life I was ever sure about," he said. "It ain't like it was with Nan. I'd follow you anywhere you went. I wouldn't give you up. I won't let nothing come between us. I quit when Nan wouldn't come with me." He paused, searching her face and finding there what he sought, and he added, "I ain't worried about the past. It's gone and done with. It's just the future that counts and we'll make it count."

He put his arms around her and she came to him, whispering, "I knew last night when you kissed me. I was afraid you didn't."

"I knew," he said, "but I couldn't tell you then. I wanted everything settled. A lot of things to be done yet, but we'll do them."

"We! Always think of it that way, Rick. Never you or me or Hatchet."

He kissed her the way a man kisses the woman he loves. She had his love and he had hers. It was more than he had ever dreamed. It was all he wanted. It was enough.

We hope that you enjoyed reading this
Sagebrush Large Print Western.
If you would like to read more Sagebrush titles,
ask your librarian or contact the Publishers:

## United States and Canada

Thomas T. Beeler, *Publisher*
Post Office Box 659
Hampton Falls, New Hampshire 03844-0659
(800) 818-7574

## United Kingdom, Eire, and
## the Republic of South Africa

Isis Publishing Ltd
7 Centremead
Osney Mead
Oxford OX2 0ES England
(01865) 250333

## Australia and New Zealand

Bolinda Publishing Pty Ltd
17 Mohr Street
Tullamarine, Victoria, 3043, Australia
1 800 335 364